Dannielle Davis has an MA in Creative Writing and a BA in Creative Writing and Film Studies at Kingston University. The inspiration for *Sun Burn* came after she spent three consecutive summers working in Ibiza from 2004-2007.

Her main influences are Quentin Tarantino, Irvine Welsh and Martina Cole.

This is her first book and she is currently writing her second book, *Ruby Skies*. She is interested in writing about strong female protagonists and the criminal underworld.

I would like to dedicate my first book to Alice, Richard and of course my mother Lorraine who never stopped believing in me.

Dannielle Davis

SUN BURN

AUSTIN MACAULEY
PUBLISHERS LTD.

A CIP catalogue record for this title is available from the British Library.

ISBN 9781786936738 (Paperback)
ISBN 9781786936745 (E-Book)
www.austinmacauley.com

First Published (2017)
Austin Macauley Publishers Ltd.
25 Canada Square
Canary Wharf
London
E14 5LQ

1

The crowd's cheers and whistles flooded over the loud *thud, thud, thud* of the music as thousands of palms lifted simultaneously in the air. "Welcome to Ibiza, baby!" Lucia shouted, taking Stacey's hand and raising it towards the airplane that descended upon the island in the powder blue sky.

The sun's rays pierced through the netted roof, shining on the faces of the revelers below as they watched the plane pass over them. The electronic bass became louder in response to the moment, reverberating through the mass of moving bodies as rainbow glitter fluttered down on them from a stilted woman whose sequinned bikini dazzled as she negotiated her way through the crowd.

Stood on a podium in the middle of the dance floor, Stacey couldn't help but smile as she observed the beautiful spectacle that was Ibiza's super club, Space, from behind her sunglasses. Despite Lucia's insistence that it was the best on the island, she'd been reluctant to attend the famous opening party. Especially when Lucia had informed her that they needed to be through the gates before 11 a.m. in order to qualify for the reduced entry fee. *What type of person goes clubbing in the morning?* She'd thought to herself as Lucia spoke excitedly about how amazing Space was and how happy she was to be taking Stacey there. Lucia had promised Stacey that if she didn't like the party, which she'd assured her would be *impossible*; they would walk straight out of the club and spend the day on the beach opposite. As always, Lucia was completely right, it was *impossible* not to like Space. The vibe was different from any club Stacey had ever been to before. Everyone was so carefree and happy, making the atmosphere so enjoyably contagious that she soon realised that bringing her beach bag as a backup had been completely unnecessary. *She wasn't going anywhere.*

Stacey watched Lucia as she danced next to her on the podium. Her caramel skin was glowing from the heat and her eyes were closed underneath her gold-framed sunglasses. She moved her arms softly up and down as her hips weaved slowly from side to side. Usually when Lucia danced, she accounted for every footstep with a militant precision but basked in the sunshine, with the heady bass filling the air, her footing was looser and more fluid and Stacey was surprised to see she had completely succumbed to the moment.

When Lucia had first suggested she come with her to Ibiza, Stacey had laughed. *What would a girl like her do in Ibiza?* Lucia had it all worked out though, she'd heard about a job going for an Assistant Make-up Artist at Amnesia. It didn't pay as well as the theatre but they'd be working so much that they wouldn't need to spend a lot and they could share a room to halve the cost. Stacey knew a chance like that would probably never present itself to her again but she wasn't free to roam like Lucia. She had ties at home, a family who relied on her, she couldn't just abandon it all for a season in Ibiza.

Lucia's eyes opened underneath her glasses and she smiled as she caught Stacey staring at her. Stacey wanted to express her gratitude towards Lucia but she knew the loud music would make it impossible for her to be heard so she reached for her hand, waves of love and happiness washing over her body as she did so. It had been three hours since Lucia and she had shared an ecstasy pill. The last time Stacey had taken drugs, her whole night had ended in complete disaster so since then she'd sworn herself off drugs and going out, indefinitely. She was glad that after Lucia's gentle persuasion she'd given it another try, she felt so free from her worries now. *It wasn't like they would be making a habit of it*, Stacey reassured herself. In forty-eight hours Lucia and she would start their jobs at Amnesia, which meant they would be required to work six, sometimes seven nights a week. This would be their last chance to really party until the end of the season. Lucia had spent the previous summer working as a podium dancer for Amnesia so she knew all about survival on the island. *First rule*, she'd told Stacey, *was to know your limits*. Even though Ibiza would be crazy, they would be responsible for holding the party together so they had to stay in control and moderate their fun. The whole idea suited Stacey just fine, she'd seen enough out of control people to last her a lifetime. Unlike most of the people who came to the island, working in Ibiza wasn't all about the partying to her.

Stacey flicked her auburn hair to the side of her, unsticking it from her wet back. Her tongue felt coarse in her mouth and she started to panic as she realised it had been a good couple of hours since she'd last drunk any water.

"Come to the bar," Lucia mouthed over the music as if reading her mind.

Stacey grabbed her bag and Lucia's hand and jumped off the podium they'd been dancing on for the last hour. It was so crowded on the dance floor, Stacey could barely see beyond where she was standing. Not that Lucia let it hold her back, with her skimpy gold bikini top and her flawless white smile, she instantly connected with the men and the women who were in their way, causing them to happily step aside to let her through. Stacey loved Lucia's confidence; she didn't shy away from situations like Stacey tended to do. She was in your face but in a good way, like a firework you couldn't help staring at.

"Come, come, baby," she said, squeezing Stacey's hand as she led her to the bar. Lucia ushered her into a space between two men as Stacey clamped onto the sticky surface of the bar, fearing that she would be sucked back into the crowd if she let go.

"Save some for later, bitchy!" Lucia warned, a smile creeping out of the corner of her mouth as Stacey downed the ice-cold water she had ordered her. Stacey stopped drinking and laughed as she took check on herself. The last two hours had been a blissful blur and now that she was slowly coming back around she started to see herself for what she was – *completely and utterly out of it.* "Ecstasy".

A roughly-shaven, dark haired man in a straw hat, had approached Lucia. His hand was linked to a blonde haired girl with huge blue eyes, skimpy denim shorts and a Hawaiian garland around her neck. Lucia nodded at the guy whose hand remained locked with the blonde girl. *What is she doing?* Stacey thought as the man leant in towards Lucia. Stacey caught a whiff of his musty skin as Lucia spoke over the music with him in Italian, the words flowing off her tongue as if she was singing. Stacey suddenly felt alienated from the conversation. She tried to nudge Lucia but she didn't react. Stacey looked around awkwardly, her eyes meeting the blonde girl whose dumbfounded expression seemed to mirror her own.

"You want that we get some pills, baby? Carry on the party?" Lucia asked, completely oblivious to Stacey's horrified look.

"I'm OK. I'm still *so* wasted," Stacey answered, hoping Lucia would notice the resistance in her voice.

Lucia ignored her and turned back to the dealer placing her hand out in front of him.

The girl reached inside her shorts, producing two white pills on her palm. Lucia put one to her mouth and licked it. Her face winced as it fizzed against her tongue. Snapping it in half, she then passed it to Stacey.

"I'm OK, really. I still feel well out of it to be honest," Stacey replied, having to shout her words over the music.

"That was *three* hours, baby. You can't still feel *that* high. *Come on;* don't make me bite it for nothing!"

Both the dealer, his girlfriend and Lucia were looking directly at Stacey as she shifted from side to side.

"It's our only party. We *have* to enjoy!"

"OK, *OK.* Give it here," Stacy said trying to look appreciative as they all watched her take the pill like a reluctant patient at a mental asylum.

"*Perfetto!* Good girl," Lucia said, winking at her as she swallowed the other half.

A strong force pushed Stacey, causing her to stumble against the bar. Regaining her balance, she searched for the culprit. There was a man with his back to her, blocking her view of the others his huge shoulders encased in a black t-shirt with the words SECURITY emblazoned across it.

He turned to the side and Stacey could see he had swooped in on the dealer and his girlfriend. Stacey froze, watching the scene unfold like you would a car crash. Her eyes flickered over to Lucia who was biting down on her lip, her eyes focused on the security guard who'd just discovered the baggie containing hundreds of white pills in the girl's shorts.

2

Stacey watched as, Lucia quickly threw the other pill on the ground, stamping on it till it crumbled into white powder on the litter-riddled floor. Another guard arrived and confronted Stacey, shouting at her in Spanish.

"I'm sorry but I'm English. I don't understand you!" Stacey shouted back. The security guard patted her down, then opened her pink shoulder bag, pulling apart her compact mirror and lipstick case with a frantic force. Some of the crowd had stopped dancing and were now transfixed as the security guard unzipped her beach bag.

"There's nothing in there," Stacey yelled, the heat rushing to her cheeks as the guard pulled out her factor fifty sunblock and two beach towels for all to see.

"Where are they?" he asked, his voice bellowing over the unrelenting bass.

Stacey shrugged her shoulders and shook her head suddenly feeling like she was on the worst trip ever as another two guards arrived, this time circling the four of them as they all stood with their hands in the air. The guard who had just searched Stacey turned his attention to Lucia who started to wave her hands around and shout in Spanish at them in protest.

Stacey wished Lucia would just co-operate, the last thing she wanted was for them to be banged up in some Spanish jail. The first guard had hold of the couple and was waiting for the other guard who was still being yelled at by Lucia. After finally managing to search her, the guard nodded his head in the direction of his colleague who escorted the man and his sobbing girlfriend into the crowd.

"You're free to go." The guard said, pointing to a space on the dancefloor, his dark brown eyes looking back and forth between Stacey and Lucia with a steely gaze. "But beware, we watch you now." He directed his last remark at Lucia who tutted and turned away from him.

Lucia waited till the guard was out of sight then looked at Stacey, her brow furrowed and her eyes wide with anger.

"Stupid security! This is Ibiza. Why the fuck are they doing that?"

Stacey didn't reply; although she felt instantly relieved that her newly found freedom was still intact, she couldn't help but feel sad for the man in the hat, the crying girl and the trouble that now awaited them. Stacey noticed a tall woman scanning the area of the bar.

She started to walk towards Stacey and Lucia with a look of desperation in her eyes. Lucia grabbed her hand, indicating for them to move away but Stacey's legs were trembling so badly she couldn't move from her spot.

"I'm sorry to bother you. I'm looking for a guy about this high with a blonde girl in tow."

Stacey registered an Australian accent as the woman indicated to a height just below her enormous breasts.

"He's wearing a straw hat and the girl he's with is my sister. They told me they would meet me by the bar but I can't find them at all. Have you seen them at all?"

Stacey couldn't hear her that well over the music but it was obvious the woman was talking about the same couple who had just been carted away.

"What she wanna do?" Lucia asked Stacey, her words hissing into her ears.

"Let's go, baby. We don't need no trouble."

"If you know something I would be really grateful." Stacey hesitated. She really didn't want to involve herself with it all but she couldn't help but feel partly responsible for the mess they were in.

"I'm sorry but they were taken by security."

Instantly Stacey saw the woman's face start to crumple. She'd lost count of all the times she'd spent pleading with strangers for the people she loved and even though she was relieved it wasn't her in that position she couldn't help the sinking feeling of guilt that clung to her. "They found the drugs. They took them both. I'm sorry. There was nothing I could do to stop it."

"Fuck, fuck, fuck!" The woman shouted, tears gathering in her blue eyes as she placed her hand over her head. "Can you wait here?"

Stacey nodded and the woman disappeared into the crowd.

"Why you always got to be the good *Samaritana*, eh? For a shitty drug dealer?" Lucia asked, pulling her hand away and pouting her lips. Realising the answer to her question, she let out a little huff and reaching for Stacey's hand she placed it back into her own.

"This is my friend, Tomas. Tomas, these are the girls who were with Christian and Liz."

A red bandanna held Tomas' greasy hair back, as streams of sweat trickled down his forehead at an alarming rate. His skin was the darkest shade of orange and his over-pumped muscles bulged out of his vest top like they wanted to explode. Stacey didn't know whether to run or stay, as she noticed the words 'SECURITY' written on his chest.

He beckoned for them to join him by the sofas, the music wasn't as loud there and Stacey appreciated the opportunity to sit down. "Can you remember what happened? What security guards took them?" the woman asked, her eyes darting from Stacey to a disinterested looking Lucia.

Stacey tried to envisage the security guards, but no matter how hard she tried she couldn't recall anything from the last ten minutes, it was as if her memory was filled with black spots.

"They found the pills on your sister. I don't know what they looked like. All I can remember is that there were two of them and they both had black hair and black T-shirts. I'm sorry."

"Well that's not a lot of help, they all wear black fucking t-shirts!"

"That is all we know OK? So it's better that you go find them and leave us alone," Lucia fired back, her chin raised defiantly towards the woman.

"One of them had a dragon tattoo up his arm, I think," Stacey blurted out as the memory announced itself like a surprise visitor in her mind.

"Ah yes, I know." Tomas' face became animated as the woman turned to him, her lip quivering.

"Don't worry, Mary, I'll sort it."

Stacey watched on in horror as Tomas put his arm around Mary, pulling her closer to him.

"How you doing anyways, apart from all this?"

Mary leant away from him, her lips curled up like she had smelt something bad.

"I'm not great, Tomas! My fucking ignoramus sister has a habit of ruining my night. I'll be happier when I know she is OK."

"Mary, *please, trust in me.* I will sort this for you, even though I don't start my shift yet that's how much you mean to me, OK? *Try not to worry*; this club has bigger things going on today. Your sister and her boyfriend will not be their top priority. It's better to let them sweat it a little. The *Policia* will not be called, so just relax." Tomas put his arm around Mary, his hungry eyes scanning her body.

"I really appreciate your help, girls. If there is anything I can do for you, just let me know." Mary's eyes fell upon Stacey's beach bag. "Why the hell are you carrying that thing about?"

"Oh yeah, that. Long story," Stacey replied feeling the blood rush to her cheeks in embarrassment.

Mary's lips formed into a small smile.

"OK. Well, as a thanks for helping me out, I could get Tomas to put it in the office for you? I can come with you then, hopefully we can see what's happening with Liz and that fucking dick Christian."

"Ah yeah, of course I'll sort it out. Just give me five," Tomas replied, his gruff tone indicating that he was not overly happy at the prospect.

Mary's brow furrowed and her lips pressed into a slim line.

"For all you know, Tomas, my sister could be half way to Ibiza nick by now. All whilst you're having your five minutes."

Tomas sweated it out for a millisecond before he reluctantly grabbed Stacey's bag.

"Come to find me later and I'll have your bag. I'll be at the front after midnight. OK?"

"OK thanks," Stacey replied as Tomas headed into the crowd, with the might that was Mary in tow.

"Thanks to God that is over," Lucia said, pulling a *Vogue* cigarette from her bag.

"Now let's go to the *Terrazza*, bitchy. I wanna forget these losers."

Lucia inhaled a long drag on her cigarette, pouted her lips and breathed a perfect hoop-shaped cloud of smoke into the air. She reached out her perfectly manicured hand to Stacey, who happily took it, comforted in the knowledge that whatever happened she would always have her best friend by her side.

3

A loud noise in the distance brought Stacey out of the darkness with a jolt. She turned her head frantically from side to side trying to gain some sort of bearing, but her vision was blurred. Her fingers slipped through the metal lid of the blue container next to her but it was as if her hands were made of rubber. The air smelt putrid, and she resisted the urge to gag. Her denim shorts were down by her ankles and twisting her neck around, she noticed a toilet behind her – the association of the two floating through her mind like a flitting butterfly.

The vibration of the music in the background caused the walls around Stacey to shake so much she thought they were going to cave in. She tried to send a message to her brain to reach the door ahead of her but there was no response. Instead she held her fingers out in the air in front of her, hypnotized by their blurred outlines.

Someone was shouting, but it seemed far off, like a distant memory of something she used to be. Another rush took over her body, lurching her forward as saliva hung from her chin like silver thread, glistening against the sterile lights. A familiar voice was calling out to her but she couldn't answer. She attempted to stand, but fell back down. Her eyes became drawn to the dirty, red tiles on the floor. There was another bang on the door but she was too out of it to move. Stacey bowed her head in submission.

"Stacey! Are you in there? Stacey!"

Stacey fought against the force that was weighing down her body and managed to push herself up. Her hands played with the lock as someone pushed against the door. She felt her body fold back down on the seat as a distorted face appeared in front of her.

There was a tickling feeling against her legs as her shorts were pulled up and she saw a cluster of white come towards her face, brushing against it like a dry sponge. Lucia's face came into focus, a white light shining from the top of her head.

"*Madonna*! I've been looking for you everywhere! One minute you are dancing, next I look and you're gone. I was so worried. I'm sorry for pushing you to take another pill *Si prega di essere OK*. Come, we need to get you out of here. Can you stand?" Lucia asked, as she put her arms around Stacey and helped her to get up.

A line of women waited by the sinks for the next available toilet. Their eyes widened as Lucia guided Stacey towards the mirrors. Lucia hoisted her onto the side, much to the annoyance of the toilet attendant, who started to moan at them only to go quiet when she noticed the state Stacey was in. Lucia peeled off Stacey's hat with the words 'Mother Trucker' printed on it and relaxed as Stacey began to cool down. A vision of her grabbing it from some man's head, flashed into Stacey's thoughts. Using s wet hand towels, Lucia dabbed Stacey's forehead and the back of her neck. Stacey turned to the mirror, shocked by her reflection. Her usually pale complexion was flushed and blotchy, her jaw was chattering against itself repeatedly and her blue eyes were almost black, her pupils were that dilated. On top of that, the eye make-up she had so meticulously applied had managed to smudge, causing two black lines to go all the way down to her cheeks. Her first reaction was to reach for the little bit of make-up she had in her bag, but even she knew she was way too high to even attempt it. Lucia wiped the black from her face and tried to brush her wet hair back with her fingers. She succeeded in removing the black but failed to make her hair look any better. After a few seconds of contemplation, she took the stolen hat and placed it back on Stacey's head, pulling the rim down so it almost covered her eyes.

"There, you don't look so bad."

"Thanks, Luce. Sorry about this."

"I should be the one who is sorry. I'm just glad you're OK. One minute you were dancing with this guy, putting his hat on, next you disappear."

Stacey screwed up her face as she tried to remember what happened after she took the hat.

"You OK to go back inside? Or do you need some more time?"

"I definitely feel a lot better," Stacey replied, wiggling her toes in front of her.

"Are you sure?"

"I think so," Stacey replied, still not sure if she would be able to stand but determined not to sit in the toilets any longer.

"OK then. *If you are sure*? Come, Eric Morillo is playing." Lucia held out her hand to Stacey and she once again took it, following her out onto the dance floor.

The number of bodies in the *Terrazza* had almost doubled from before and Stacey had become unlocked from Lucia by the sheer force of the crowd. She trailed behind erratically as her footing became more and more unstable. Pushed back and forth, she lost her balance and fell into the bodies in front of her. Unable to take Stacey's weight the people around her backed away and she plummeted towards the ground as the rest of the swarming crowd's heavy feet kicked against her.

4

"Grab on will ya. Take my arm. We need to get you out of here."

Stacey heard a man's voice speaking to her in a deep Liverpudlian accent and before she had a chance to look up two strong hands reached out to her, lifting her off the ground. "Can you stand up?" her rescuer asked her, grabbing her tighter and ushering her to a space against the wall. "Wow! You were nearly a goner then."

Stacey was still holding onto the stranger who'd saved her, his citrusy cologne and warm breath comforted her as the room spun around them.

"*Hello?* What's your name? *Hello?* You are far too pretty to be messing yourself up like this, girl."

His brown eyes met Stacey's and for a split second, she felt the compelling urge to reach out and kiss him.

"Where's your mates, love?"

He slowly placed her feet on the floor as Stacey tried to regain her stance.

"I don't know. I don't know. I lost her." Stacey attempted to search for Lucia, but her legs buckled beneath her and once again the man steadied her.

"What are you doing? Sit here and relax, I'm gonna search for your friend. Wait here, OK?"

Stacey allowed herself to relax as the stranger lowered her to a space on the ground.

Giving her a lingering look, he disappeared into the vast mass of bodies. She slumped back down to the ground against the wall, it felt good to get off her feet and she started to feel herself coming back around. People were staring at her but she couldn't care less, all she had to do was wait till her hero came back and everything would be OK.

"It's you! Thank God!" Lucia appeared in front of her, her hands feeling around Stacey's face. "You have to stop scaring me like this, OK?"

"Think she's had one too many disco biscuits love! Lucky I was close by, or she would have been flattened. It's manic in here tonight. Opening parties all the same, gotta keep your wits about ya."

Stacey was still lying on the ground, she was so smashed she didn't feel the slightest bit of embarrassment as they both examined her. "She deffo needs to go home. The security is ruthless in here. She'll be kicked out in no time if they see her like that."

"Thank you, yes, we need to get a taxi. For sure she needs to go home." Stacey listened to Lucia and her gorgeous rescuer talk about her like she wasn't even there, the saliva dribbling down her chin. She couldn't help but think to herself that they sounded like the parents she'd never had.

"I couldn't believe it. One minute I'm standing at the bar, next thing I spot *her*, taking a dive into the crowd."

Stacey tried to reply, but it was as if she'd reverted back to infancy, all she could manage was a gurgle.

"If there ever was an advert not to do drugs, eh! Thankfully, it's nothing some water and a bit of shut eye won't fix!"

Her rescuer lifted her up, carrying her across the dance floor as the scenery around her unfolded itself in a host of fuzzy images. Despite being more wasted than she had ever been before, all she could think about was the goose pimples that had come up over her body as he carried her over the dance floor.

"She can't be having that bad a time! She's smiling away."

Stacey's rescuer placed her gently on the red cushions of a sofa and suddenly she felt very drawn to the man who had stopped her being stampeded on. Her eyes flickered over to Lucia who face was all smiles as she thanked the man. As wasted as she was Stacey was sure she noticed Lucia blush as she talked to him. Not that she could blame her, with his sandy coloured hair muscular physique and, a jawline that would give Brad

Pitt a run for his money, she'd defy any woman not to get flustered in his company.

"Hopefully she'll be OK now. Fucked up bitchie, say, thank you." Stacey raised her head from her slumped position on the couch.

"Thannkskk."

The man smiled.

"That's all right, take care of yourselves. And no more drugs for you!"

Stacey nodded in agreement, her eyes lingering on his. She could have sworn something had passed between them but before she had a chance to ponder over it, he was gone, blending into the crowd almost as quickly as he appeared. Stacey wanted to cry out to him, to tell him she thought she was falling in love with him but luckily for the smidgen that was left of her dignity she was too wasted to speak and all she could manage was a whimper in his direction.

5

"First we have to find Tomas with our bag. Then, we gotta get a taxi back to San Antonio and get you into the bed ready for tomorrow."

Stacey followed Lucia into the area outside, grateful for a guidance.

"Did you see him?" Stacey asked Lucia, causing her to stop in her tracks.

"Who you talking about?"

"You know who, Nico. Did you see him?"

"No I didn't see him. I saw his friend, Salvatore in the VIP. He wanted me to join him but I was too busy searching for you."

"Oh shit, sorry."

"No, don't worry it's not a problem. I didn't know if Nico was there. Anyways it's better that I didn't stay, Salvatore can be too much sometimes. The way he looks at me. I'm sure if Nico and I didn't have something he would try with me. Men like that you don't want to be serious with. They only want possessions not people. He wanted to tell me something about Nico but I didn't want to hear it. I thought I wanted to know why he was such a bastardo last summer but actually I don't. I'm so done with that man and any of the stupid excuses he has."

"Good on you, babe. You know no matter what happens you've got me by your side. We don't need any men messing us about," Stacey announced, grabbing Lucia's arm.

"This is true bitchy you are so much better than a stupid Italian try-to-be gangster!"

"For *sure!*" Stacey straightened herself out and looked triumphantly into the night's sky. "Even though my body is aching all over, I had the best time. Thank you so much for persuading me to come!"

"Me too, baby. You are so funny when you're fucked up. I've never even seen you drink before."

"Well I won't be letting myself get in a state like that again in a hurry!"

Lucia and Stacey giggled to each other as they walked towards the main exit gate.

"That's him, isn't it?" Stacey asked spotting a guard standing against the fire exit at the back of club shepherding the crowd away from the gate. His body was tensed up and his eyes seemed to glaze over as Stacey and Lucia got closer to him.

"This is no entry. You have to use the other exit."

"Excuse me but…"

"No entry," he said interrupting Lucia. "Use the other exit."

"It's OK, just leave it, Luce, he obviously doesn't remember us," Stacey said, not wanting to argue over a beach bag she purchased for three pounds from Primark.

Lucia shrugged her off and turned to Tomas with a look of determination in her eyes.

"Excuse me but you have our bag, and we are not going until we get it back."

"Me? Are you crazy? Does it look like I have your bag?" Tomas snarled at Lucia as Stacey tried to drag her away.

"Your name is Tomas, right?" she asked as Tomas screwed up his face.

"Yeah, so?"

"My friend gave you her bag," Lucia replied, the frustration clear in her voice.

"I don't know what you're talking about but you can't stand here. *If* you gave it to security then maybe your bag is in the office."

A zombie-like crowd was starting to form behind them and Stacey could see Tomas was starting to lose his patience.

"Where is the office?"

"Over there, but you're not allowed there. Can everyone move back! This is no entry!"

His jaw started to clench as he shouted at the people behind, inches away from Stacey's face.

On closer inspection, Stacey could see his pupils were dilated and his eyes were wide, it was obvious he was wired.

"Look, we gave our bag to a girl named Mary," Stacey said, exasperated by the whole conversation.

"You know Mary? Why didn't you say? Oh my God! *I know you.* Yes, yes, I put your bag, wait a minute. Sorry, *Chicas.*"

Tomas whistled to another security guard. He spoke to his colleague in Spanish, before leaving to get the bag. It seemed like an eternity before he came back, Stacey's floral beach bag in hand.

"Sorry, *Chicas*, someone had moved it, so wasn't easy to find. Next time you come, ask for me, I get you free entry. Can you tell Mary I say 'Hi' please?"

Stacey took the beach bag and smiled wearily in Tomas' direction.

"No! It can't be! No! It's one-thirty baby! We have been in Space for fourteen hours!"

"What? No? I can't believe it! It literally felt like minutes! Probably 'cause I was so wasted but still fourteen hours how the hell did that even happen?"

"I told you it's the bestest, most craziest party you have ever been to! Come let's get back, we have a big day tomorrow."

"Bed is sounding so good to me right now!"

"Me too, baby!" Lucia exclaimed as they walked towards the taxi rank.

Stacey couldn't wait to go to sleep and wake up feeling normal again. She had never felt more tiered and drained, even her beach bag felt like it was full of bricks which was funny considering it only had a bottle of sun block and a couple of towels inside. So far Lucia and herself had hit Ibiza with a bang and it had been amazing but that was it now. Working in Ibiza was all about staying in control, working hard and saving money and Stacey wouldn't want it any other way,

Amnesia

1

"You're pretty for an English girl. Not many red haired girls either. Interesting."

Stacey's eyes fell upon the piles of CVs and pictures, sprawled across Jorge's desk.

"So what makes you think you can work in a place like this? Ibiza isn't some theatre in London. Ibiza is tough. I have hundreds of girls send these CVs. They all think they can survive out here but most don't last beyond their first night."

Stacey could feel the heat start to rise to her cheeks as Jorge examined her with his black-coffee eyes. Her body had started to shake and her words felt like they were trapped inside of her. Taking a deep breath, she willed herself to answer as succinctly as she could.

"I know it won't be easy but I'm not the type of person to fall at the first hurdle. I am passionate about what I do and dedicated as well. You won't have any problems with me."

Jorge pushed his long curly black hair from his face as he flicked through her CV.

"Stacey is extremely talented. Not only is she the best I've seen, she is an artist. I wouldn't have anyone else make me up."

Stacey did her best to smile at Lucia's compliment as the pounding in her head continued.

"Artist or not, this place takes stamina, you need to stay on top of your game."

Stacey sat up straight and double blinked her eyes as Lucia sympathized with Jorge.

With his long hair and tight vest top, Stacey had assumed he would be a softy but it was obvious, after a few seconds, that he was anything but. It helped that Jorge clearly fancied Lucia. He was constantly flicking through her portfolio, sticking out his chest and staring at her with his intense eyes.

"Amnesia is the *only* place to be in Ibiza," Lucia said, her lips pouting as she spoke.

And everyone knows it's because of your management." She purred out the last words and Jorge smiled, soaking up the compliment.

"Thank you, my *Bella Ballerina*, with your talent and dedication you are easy to manage."

As long as you stay away from the bad boys this season. I don't want a repeat of what happened last year. Has Lucia told you about my drugs policy?"

"No getting wasted whilst we work?"

"That's right. Even our Ballerina had a hard time following that rule." He turned to Lucia, whose face started to redden.

"You know it wasn't my fault! I wasn't in a good place with that *basta*, Nico, and I found it hard to say no. Everybody always wants to party with the star."

It was said tongue-in-cheek but the tension between Lucia and Jorge over this matter was obvious and it made Stacey wonder how bad she'd actually been. Lucia hadn't mentioned any slip ups with regard to her work but she had spoken about the hurt she'd experienced with the way Nico had treated her.

"I know and I understood but it's not going to happen again. I need my staff fresh and clean and ready for work."

"It won't be a problem," Stacey replied, the thought of going crazy again like last night making her feel queasy.

"I take it this is this your first time in Ibiza?"

"Yes," Stacey answered, her voice still shaky.

"And how are you finding it?"

Once again, she felt his dark eyes bore into her and squirmed in her seat as she responded.

"I've only been here a day but I can see it's a place that needs professional people behind the scenes to keep it going."

"Hmm. You definitely are giving the right answers but as I've said, I've heard thousands of promises. The proof is always in the action. It says here, you're a qualified Make-up Artist?"

"Yes. I graduated in April."

"Not long then but you must be good if Lucia has brought you with her all the way to Ibiza."

"I'd like to think so," Stacey replied, knowing now was not the time to act modest.

"And you're looking to become part of the Amnesia team?"

"Yes. I would love that." Stacey felt herself getting excited at the thought of all the beautiful dancers whose make-up she would be doing.

"We do already have a Make-up Artist who has been working with us for over ten years."

Lucia huffed and Jorge smiled.

"I know our star here doesn't really get on with her."

"She makes me look like a drag queen!"

Stacey held back her laughter, noticing that Jorge's face remained serious.

"I could look into appointing you as her assistant. Her name is Carmen and I think she is very skilled at what she does. Maybe she could teach you some things?"

Lucia huffed again and Stacey blocked her out. As much as Lucia could get away with being obnoxious, this was her big break and she needed to look humble.

"Although..." Stacey felt his eyes on her again. *What was he looking at?* Anxious that Jorge was about to change his mind, she spoke up. "I don't mind working under someone. It's fine. Carmen sounds like she knows what she's doing. You're right, I could definitely learn from her."

Lucia smiled at her, indicating to Stacey that she'd said the right thing.

"OK then. Good stuff. It says here you're English. That explains your lack of colour."

Jorge laughed at his own joke and Stacey made herself smile. He wasn't the first person who had commented on her paleness. Matched with her freckles and ginger hair she had always been the brunt of other people's jokes but luckily over the years she'd learnt to rise above it.

"And you're twenty-one, just a little bit on the young side for such responsibility. Are you sure you can handle what Ibiza has to offer?"

Stacey felt both Jorge's and Lucia's eyes bore into her. Willing her voice not to break she held Jorge's glare with her own and continued,

"I may only be twenty-one but I have experienced a lot more than most girls my age. So you won't have to worry about me not being able to handle myself. I've been looking after myself since I was a child and will not let you down."

Both Lucia and Jorge looked visibly shocked by her answer.

"OK, well seems I misjudged you, Miss Mears. If you're as good as you say then you should fit in pretty well around here." Jorge had her CV in his hands and once again started to flick through it. "So you met each other at work then?"

"Yes, *Bello*, as I told you, she is very talented an artist! I had to take her for myself!"

Stacey nodded and smiled with clenched teeth, hopeful that Jorge would never have to learn the truth of how they had really met.

2

Stacey pulled her hoodie tighter around her as she
walked towards her home. She had been perfecting her
styling at the college salon since she finished class at
four and it was now dark outside. Unlocking the door of
her mum's three bedroom flat, she was welcomed by the
sound of silence. Her mum and brother were out and
Stacey breathed a sigh of relief. As per usual the flat
resembled a squat, her mum had obviously been on one
of her benders. She shuddered as the memory of last
month's mice infestation entered her thoughts. Even
though the council had fumigated the house and laid
several traps with the assurance they wouldn't come
back, she still wasn't entirely convinced they'd gone for
good. She grabbed a black sack from the kitchen and
threw in the beer cans, takeaway boxes, full to the brim
ashtrays and empty vodka bottles. Gathering all the dirty
glasses and cutlery she placed them in the sink and
started to run some hot water on top. She opened the
curtains and the windows as wide as possible and doused
the furnishings with the vanilla and magnolia air

freshener she'd purchased from the pound shop. Pleased with her make over, she walked upstairs. She froze in the hallway when she noticed that the padlock on her door had been completely screwed off.

"Oh no, please, not my room."

Unable to look, she placed her hand over her eyes and pushed the door open with her foot. She willed herself to peel back her hand from her face and slowly opened her eyes.

Her normally neat room had been pulled apart. Books had been thrown from the shelves and her clothes had been scattered across the floor. Dumped on the bed was her savings tin, it had been completely emptied. Fighting back the tears, Stacey hurled it across the room as her phone vibrated in her pocket. It was the pub down the road, she'd given the landlord her number for when her mum decided to go on one of her 'crazies'. It was better than her getting nicked; the last time that had happened she'd hit the arresting officer and ended up in prison for six months. It had caused a disastrous ripple effect on their lives: Stacey had been put into a women's shelter and her brother ended up on the streets where he developed a drug habit. That was two years ago and needless to say it had been the worst time of Stacey's life.

"Stace? It's me, Sid. Let's just say your mum is having one of her moments and I need you to come get her sharpish."

"Oh God! OK, no problem. Thanks for ringing me. I'll be right down."

"Alright, love. If you could hurry it will be really appreciated, she has just thrown a chair across the room. We've tried to kick her out but she's turned savage."

"OK, OK, I'll come now. Thanks, Sid." Stacey cringed as she heard her mum screaming in the background.

"You got five minutes love, otherwise I'll have no choice but to call the Old Bill."

Stacey sprinted most of the way to the pub and was relieved when she got there to see her mum, propped up against the wall outside, muttering to herself. She was wearing a pair of pink grubby leggings that were so old they'd practically gone see-through and her greasy greying hair was hanging down the side of her gaunt face in a massive knot. Back in the day, her mum had actually been a beauty. It was her relationships with men which had put her on the road to ruin. It'd all started with Stacey's dad, who'd abandoned her whilst pregnant, stealing all her savings on his way out. Then her brother's dad who beat her within an inch of her life and took off with her best friend. After that, it was just one disastrous relationship after another, each one leaving her mum a little bit more broken. It was no secret her mum had problems with both alcohol and drugs. Stacey had taken her to countless rehab meetings and clinics but it was a losing battle. In the end, she'd had no choice but to give up on her fantastical notion that her mum would ever stay sober. If she was honest with herself, she was continually surprised that her mother was still alive, the amount of crap she piled into her body. Her once beautiful smile was now practically toothless and Stacey knew her body was covered in sores. On top of that, her organs had now started to pack up which meant continual visits to the hospital whenever her mum decided to overdo it. Despite all the warnings, she still carried on taking, somewhere behind those dead eyes there was a fire that still needed to be fuelled. Being her daughter and the only one capable of keeping an eye out for her, Stacey felt like it was her job to look after her until eventually the fire went out. *After all, who could just give up on their mother?*

"Oh, if it isn't fucking-shit-don't-stink, ungrateful bitch, herself."

"You all right, Mum. You coming home now?"

Stacey really wanted to ask about the missing money but knew it would only make things worse. Instead, she held out her hand to her mum and prayed for co-operation.

"I ain't going nowhere with you," her mother answered, burying her head into her hands.

"Come on, we need to get you home. Take my hand, please."

"Fuck off!"

"I'll buy you a packet of fags."

Her mum lifted her head up.

"I want a bluey as well."

Stacey knew that her mum meant Tennents Super; as rank as it was, it was the fuel that powered her messed up life.

"All right but you have to come now."

Stacey's mum took her hand but instead of pulling herself up, she pulled Stacey down with such a force, she came crashing down on the ground. Her mum started to laugh as Stacey tasted the blood in her mouth from her cut lip. Holding back her tears, she stood up, brushed herself down and started to walk off.

"Guess you won't be needing your *Bluey* or your fags then?" she called back to her mum, who pushed herself up and tried stagger after her. She waited with her hand out until her mum's bony fingers locked with hers. Her mother was leaning against her like she was a crutch. Fearing she would be pulled onto the gravel again, Stacey let her grip go. She watched in horror as her mother tumbled onto one of the doorsteps of the newly-built town houses.

"No, Mum! Not here! Come on! We have to get you home!"

Stacey's mum leant forward and vomited on the doorstep. Stacey hoped and prayed that whoever lived at the address was out for the night and that the vomiting would be over quickly. The damage to her mum's liver meant the vomiting could go on for days if she didn't receive some sort of treatment. *Great, another night at the hospital,* Stacey thought to herself as she rubbed her mum's back.

The door opened and the light inside illuminated the step where Stacey and her mum were crouched. Stacey wished she could just run away and leave her mum where she was, but as per usual she was bound by blood and duty to a woman who couldn't care less about who or what she affected on her path to destruction.

"What's happened? Is she OK?" The woman standing in the doorframe was in her mid-twenties and dressed in a black silk dressing gown, black silk bottoms and pink fluffy slippers. Her concerned face was tanned yet make-up free and Stacey instantly felt guilty for rousing her from what had obviously been a relaxing night in.

"I'm sorry, she has drunk too much and decided to pass out on your doorstep. I've tried to move her but she's having none of it. I'm going to get her in the recovery position before she chokes. I'll call an ambulance and then we'll be out of your way. Sorry."

Rather than be annoyed that there was a drunken stranger now passed out on her doorstep, the woman leant down and helped Stacey lift her mum from the pile of sick and onto her side.

"I better call that ambulance. She has a liver defect and needs to go to the hospital."

The woman's beautiful face screwed up as she looked from Stacey to her mother.

"She's been drinking?" she asked, as Stacey noticed her accent.

"Yes, I'm afraid she doesn't care about all that."

"Fuck off, you fucking cunts," her mother mumbled, spitting on the ground.

"Charmed I'm sure," Stacey said, turning to the woman, who looked like she was trying to suppress a nervous grin.

"Who is she?" the woman enquired, with a mixture of concern and disbelief.

Stacey took a long breath before she answered.

"She's my mum. Unfortunately."

"I ain't your fucking mother!"

For a split second the woman looked visibly shocked. Then regaining her composure, she indicated to the open door of her home.

"Does she want to come inside?"

"I better call an ambulance. Mum, do you want to wait inside?"

"Fuck off!"

"Mum! God I'm so sorry."

The woman screwed up her face and stared at Stacey's mum as she retched onto the doorstep again.

"Why does she drink when she has this problem?"

"She's an alcoholic, which means I'm always in the hospital with her. It's just annoying because I have an important exam tomorrow and really didn't need to spend my night sitting with her in A and E. Anyway, sorry, you don't need to hear all my problems."

"No, don't be. Do you want to wait inside and call the ambulance? I can make you a hot drink."

"I better not leave her, just in case but thank you," Stacey answered, putting her hoodie around her mum.

"Get the fuck off me!" Stacey's mum reached out and struck her on the cheek as the mortified woman looked on.

"Are you OK? *Madonna*! She is crazy! Please come inside, you don't deserve that."

Stacey shivered as she held her now throbbing face. Her mum retched again, this time using Stacey's hoodie to wipe the sick from her mouth.

"Yeah I'm fine and yes she is completely insane. You know I will take you up on your offer if you don't mind. I would love a coffee especially as it now looks like I'm in for a long night."

The woman's apartment was so immaculate and modern Stacey couldn't help but stare wistfully at the clean carpets and polished sides as the woman beckoned her into the kitchen.

"Your place is beautiful, wow."

"Ah thank you, I like to keep it organized. I'm Lucia, by the way."

"Stacey. Once again, I'm sorry."

"Please stop to say this. No one's parents are perfect. It's not your fault."

"Thanks, but she is my responsibility whether I like it or not. I better call an ambulance, hopefully we can be in and out quite quickly although I very much doubt it."

"What are you studying?" Lucia asked, as she reached inside her cupboard and produced a small silver kettle and a round tin with the words *Lavazza* written on the side.

"I'm training to be a make-up artist. Well I was. If I don't go to this exam tomorrow that's me out."

"Do you have to go with her?" Lucia asked, as she scooped the coffee into the silver kettle. "It doesn't seem like she wants you there."

Stacey peered out the kitchen window at her mother who was still slumped on the ground.

"I can't just leave her. I'm all she has in this world."

Lucia filled the kettle with water and let out an understanding sigh. Stacey took out her phone and rang the emergency services, Lucia's words echoing through her mind.

"Right, the ambulance won't be long, so don't let us ruin your night anymore. I'll just wait outside till they arrive."

"Oh it's no bother. It's my night off and in fact it's good to have some company. I don't know that many people in this area."

"Well I'm not sure you want to either! Wow, is that you? Are you a dancer?" Stacey pointed to the photo of Lucia in a tutu.

"Yes, I used to be a professional ballerina back in Italy. I came to London two years ago and now I dance in musicals. Have you heard of Miss Saigon?"

"I think so. You dance in that?"

"At the moment yes. Have you been to many musicals?"

"Me? No! Musicals are for posh people. Not that I wouldn't want to or anything."

"You want to come to see it? I can get tickets?"

"Wow, are you sure?"

"Of course! It's no problem. But just you, OK?" Lucia indicated to her doorstep and Stacey felt her cheeks flush.

"Yeah of course."

"There is one condition, though."

"What's that?"

"Don't go to the hospital. You have a very important day tomorrow and if you fail it's going to mess up your life. She doesn't even know who you are. Please don't think I'm being horrible, it's just sometimes you have to do what's right for you."

The ambulance pulled up outside but Stacey didn't move.

"Think about it, do you want a life for yourself? Or do you want to give it to your mamma?" It had never occurred to Stacey that it was OK to just let go. Ever since she could remember she'd been her mum's carer but what Lucia was saying was right, if she stood by her now she'd be sacrificing her own dreams. As hard as it was, maybe it was time to put her own needs first.

3

"So now we celebrate!"

Stacey looked at Lucia, her eyes wide with terror.

"No baby. Not like that. What you think? I'm an animal? No, we go to eat." Lucia turned to the taxi driver. "Café del Mar, *gracias*."

"What's Café del Mar?"

"It's a restaurant overlooking the sea. It close to our hotel, you will love it!"

"It's next to the sea?"

"Yes, baby. I know you wanted to go to the beach but I thought we could eat something first. You know, make us feel human again."

"Oh I can wait for the beach just being near the water is enough. The last time I saw the sea was about four years ago and it was bloody raining!"

"Four?" Lucia didn't hide her shock. "Well, baby, you are in for a treat. Café del Mar is situated in one of my favourite parts of the island. People gather from all over to watch the…"

Stacey didn't hear what Lucia was saying, as soon as she'd got out of the taxi, the salty spray of the sea air had filled her lungs and beckoned her towards it. As she walked down the hill, past the apartment complexes and hotels, the horizon started to unfold itself in front of her. To her delight, she could now clearly see the crystal blue Mediterranean water as it lapped gently onto the shore below and the glimmers of gold that seemed to dance on the waves from the oversized sun above. To the right of her, there was a small sandy beach with a cluster of sunbathers and on the opposite side; there was a long curve of coastline with hotels towering over individual beaches enclosed by rocks. Several boats were cast out and Stacey smiled to herself as she heard music coming from the one filled with swaying bodies.

"It's beautiful, no?"

Stacey nodded, unable to peel her eyes away from the breath-taking panorama in front of her.

"It's the most beautiful place I have ever seen." With the lack of sleep and everything she'd been through in the last forty-eight hours, Stacey couldn't help the tears of relief that trickled down her face.

"Shh, don't cry, baby. We here now and it is only going to get better! Now you must be hungry because I am starving. Let's go get some food."

With its predominantly white and blue exterior, Café del Mar created a feeling of tranquillity that was reinforced by the music being played from the large speakers situated around the bar. The soothing melodic compositions seemed as if they were naturally in time with the waves that gently crashed on the rocks beneath them. The ambiance of the place had a serene effect on all those around it; Men and women all of ages dressed in loose fitting clothing sauntered past them, their faces happy and carefree. Stacey's eyes fell upon the deeply tanned market sellers on the beach below, offering massages, handcrafted jewellery and henna tattoos.

They appeared so blissful and content with their lives in Ibiza, she knew she'd done the right thing coming here for the season. She spotted a couple of promoters wearing Pacha t-shirts just past the bar but unlike the ones she'd seen in the West End, who hassled the tourists as they walked past; these ones seemed a lot more relaxed. Taking a deep breath in, Stacey let out a sigh of pure contentment.

"You like it here?" Lucia asked, laughing at the dopey smile that had taken over her face.

"Is it that easy to see?" Stacey replied, her eyes falling on the sparkling white interior of Café del Mar.

"You want to sit inside, my love?"

"As stunning as it is, I would rather sit outside."

Lucia smiled at her request and they chose a table directly overlooking the sea.

"As I was trying to tell you before you ran away. Every night, people gather here for the sunset. It's the best view on the island," Lucia recounted wistfully, her eyes falling on the beach below.

"That sounds amazing. I've never seen a proper sunset."

"No *problemo*. We can come tonight if you want?"

Stacey nodded vigorously, feeling like she could burst with happiness. She was a million miles from her old, stressed-filled life and as she sat back on her chair facing the magnificent sea, she realised she'd never been more content.

Thirty minutes, a pizza and two cocktails later, Lucia turned to a sleepy Stacey.

"Do you wanna that we go to the beach after this and rest?"

"Oh yeah, as long as it involves plenty of resting, I'm there!"

"OK first we have to go back to the room and get our towels. Then we can go to the beach, get some sun and then have a *siesta*."

"Sounds perfect to me. I've got to grab my sun cream out of the bag anyway."

"Yes, you need to be careful, baby, you don't wanna get sunburn."

"No way! I had it once in the summer and it was so excruciating! Us gingers are definitely not made for the heat!"

There was a pause as both Lucia and Stacey looked out onto the sea.

"Look, babe, I know I keep saying it but I just wanted to thank you for everything you have done for me."

Lucia's expression was hidden behind her glasses as she waved her hand into the air.

"Baby, really, you don't have to thank me. I am so glad I can help you. I knew I had to make you realise that you need to get away from her; like I had to get away from mine."

Stacey thought back to the night she'd first realised that not everything had been so perfect in Lucia's life. It was three weeks after Lucia and she had first met. She'd turned up to work late and was devastated to see Lucia getting her make-up done by someone else.

"Where were you? The show is about to start!" Stacey's heart felt so heavy with shame, she couldn't bring herself to tell Lucia the reason why.

"Are you just gonna stand there? Where is your make up kit?"

"I'm sorry, Lucia, but I'm quitting. You deserve someone better than me and my problems." Stacey looked to the ground as the tears ran freely from her eyes.

"What are you saying?" Lucia jumped down from her stool and comforted Stacey.

"It's my mum, she stole my kit, to pay for her drug debts."

"No, I can't believe."

"Well she did. You know what hurts the most? She knew how much that meant to me but she just doesn't care. I'm doomed, Lucia, you don't want me around you, I'll bring you nothing but bad luck."

"Don't say that amore, please."

"Come on, I'm dreaming here, look at you. You're this big star, why do you want someone like me around?"

"I can't hear this bullshit a second more. You are not the only one who has suffered in their life because of their parents, When I was a ballerina in Milano, I was only forty kilos, I suffered from black outs and my periods had completely stopped. In the end, I couldn't even perform a pirouette. Do you know why I was like this? My mamma, she believed that eating was not professional in the industry and forced me to starve myself. That's why I runaway and quit ballet. I still feel bad for leaving her but sometimes you have to do what's right for you. Now if you'll let me, I'll lend you the money for a new kit, you can keep it here and pay me off with your wages."

"Wow, I never would have realised, you seem so together. I'm sorry that happened to you."

"I need you, Stacey, more than you think. Plus, there is no quitting."

That night, Stacey watched from the sidelines as Lucia performed. Instead of seeing the perfect dancer with no worries, she now saw an artist whose every step was conjured from somewhere deep inside of her. For the first time, she realised that even the most outwardly perfect person could be hiding a sad story and to let it define you, was like letting it win. Instead of waiting for the storms to pass, she, like Lucia, must learn to dance in the rain.

4

It was nearly four in the afternoon by the time Stacey and Lucia got back to the hotel.

Once inside their room, Stacey headed to the balcony that overlooked the harbour, eager to get a glimpse of their surroundings in the daylight hours.

Last night, after Lucia and she had dragged themselves in from Space, Stacey had come out on the balcony to still herself before bed. She'd watched as rowdy groups of tourists harassed by even rowdier PRs staggered towards the West End all whilst a non-descript thud emanated from each bar. Scuttling back to her bed in horror, she'd decided never to visit the West End. She was thankful that during the day the West End was a different place. No crowds, no PR's, no loud music. *Thank God for hangovers,* Stacey thought to herself as her eyes fell upon the sandy beach and the harbour to her right.

"You ready yet, bitchy?" Lucia called from inside the room, breaking Stacey from her thoughts.

"One sec, just got to grab my bag."

Stacey reached under the bed, she hadn't had a chance to empty her bag since Space and as she pulled it towards her she noticed it still felt quite heavy.

"What the hell?" Her hand shook as it hovered over the white package next to her sun cream.

"Shit! Lucia! You better come look at this!"

Lucia walked towards the bag and joined Stacey from behind, dropping to her knees.

"*Porca Madonna*! *Catso voi*! My God! Is it real?" Lucia's eyes were wide with shock and she had turned so pale, it looked like she might faint.

"I think it's cocaine," Stacey said, stating the obvious. "A lot of cocaine. Fuck!"

Lucia took a deep breath and started pacing the room.

"Don't touch it Stacey. We don't know who it belongs to." Lucia's hands were shaking as she took two cigarettes from her bag, offering one to Stacey. Neither of them spoke as they dragged on their cigarettes and stared at the bag before them.

"Whoever this belongs to is definitely going to be looking for it," Stacey said, rubbing her forehead with her hands. "The last time we had the bag was in Space. It must have been put in there then."

"That man. What 'is name? The one who gave us the bag?"

"The sweaty guy with the bandana? I think it was Tomas. What was it he said to us?"

"Oh yeah, something about the bag being moved and that he couldn't find it at first. That was a bit dodgy. Why would someone move our bag? And why fill it with a shit load of coke?"

Lucia lit another cigarette and exhaled the smoke above their heads.

"Whoever it belongs to is not gonna be happy. We have to get it back. We could be in a lot of trouble if we don't."

"I know, babe, but what can we do? It's not like we can go to Space and just hand it in."

"Why not? It's better it not with us. Let's go to Space and find Tomas, maybe we can try to speak to him."

"And what are we going to say, Luce? *Hey, you know our bag? Well it has all this cocaine in and it's not ours.* What if he doesn't have a clue whose it is, yet he takes it anyway and whoever it belongs to, finds us? There was a guy on our estate. This gang was using his nan's lock up to stash their drugs. He found the drugs and took them for himself. He thought he got away with it, until he sold some to someone who knew the gang. They weren't happy especially when he didn't have the drugs. They sawed off his toe! I used to hate watching him struggle across the estate but that's the laws of the street. You don't mess with the big guys. Hence why we need to put this back into the hands of the owner as quickly as possible."

Lucia translated the words, her eyes widened as the realisation of what Stacey had just said dawned on her.

"You're right. *Madonna*! What we gonna do? They're gonna find us. They're probably looking now. We are not hard to find. A dancer at Amnesia and a red haired English! *Catso*!" Lucia jumped up and locked the door, turning to the window she looked out of it for a brief second then pulled the curtains across.

"Turn the light on! I can't see a thing!"

The light flicked on and Lucia's wide eyes meet Stacey's from across the room.

"You need to sit down and try to relax. It's going to be OK. We will sort this."

Lucia didn't respond, instead she sat next to Stacey on the floor, tucked her hands into her knees and started to rock back and forth. Stacey noted to keep the horror stories to herself from now on. Unlike herself, Lucia hadn't grown up in a place where drugs and violence were an almost daily occurrence.

"Try not to panic OK, Luce. If they haven't come yet and it's been twenty-four hours since we were in Space then at least we know they don't know where we live so for now, we have time." Stacey suddenly felt suffocated by the walls. "We need to get out of here though. Get some fresh air and think about what we are going to do. I don't want to stay in this room, do you?"

Lucia was breathing in and out deeply with her eyes closed. Stacey had never seen her so worked up before.

"OK. You're right. Let's hide the stuff and go to the beach. Maybe we think better when we there."

"OK, good," Stacey said, feeling strange that she was taking the lead. After examining every crevice in the room, she found a perfect place in the back of the wardrobe where the panel had come loose. She crammed the beach bag (minus the towels and sun cream) down the dusty crevice, making sure to put the panel back into its original slot.

"No one would think to look there."

"Yes it's good, baby," Lucia agreed, the colour starting to return to her cheeks.

Stacey placed her beach stuff in Lucia's bag and followed her out the door. Both of them looked around anxiously as they stepped into the empty corridor. Breathing a sigh of relief when she realised it was empty, Stacey walked down the stairs, happy to be getting away from the room and the copious amount of cocaine hidden inside.

5

Stacey stayed close to Lucia as she guided them across the promenade next to San Antonio's harbour. Her eyes didn't linger on the scenery around her, instead she kept a lookout for anyone around them acting suspiciously. They walked straight for five minutes until they reached the double roundabout that signified the end of the walkway. There was a small sandy beach and across the road two nightclubs that faced each other. One was in the shape of a glass pyramid, the words, Es Paradis, signposted across it and the other was more a square building with a cloud shaped sign with the word, Eden, written on it.

The beach was packed with sunbathers, none of whom looked up at them as they approached. Stacey searched for an available space not too close to anyone. The beach goers seemed a lot wilder here, compared to the bohemian sun seekers at Café del Mar.

Loud music from numerous portable stereos was being played, making it impossible to tell one song from the other and topless girls, with what looked suspiciously like last night's make-up smudged round their faces, cavorted with guys in football shorts sporting shockingly awful tattoos. It was obvious most of them were British by the way they acted with that typical Saturday-night-in-town mentality she had witnessed when retrieving her mum from one of her late-night benders. The noise they were making was so distracting that Stacey would have wanted to go to another beach had they not needed to be incognito.

"Shall we find a space?" Stacey asked Lucia, who hadn't said a thing since they arrived.

Lucia nodded, her expression hidden behind her oversized sunglasses. Stacey found them a spot near the sea. Lucia and she sat in silence facing the lapping water, neither of them removed their clothes. Stacey felt grounded to the spot, the severity of the situation dawning on her in waves which were becoming stronger by the second. Lucia lit another cigarette; Stacey felt like she needed one just to calm her nerves yet her mouth had gone so dry she couldn't bring herself to smoke. She examined the people around her, looking for anyone who didn't fit in but everyone looked too off their heads to be of danger to them.

"It's a lot of drugs," Stacey said, as quietly as possible. Lucia came out of her trance and faced her, none of her usual sparkle was there and it unnerved Stacey to see it.

"I know, baby. I know," she said, taking a deep drag of her cigarette. "How much do you think is there?"

"Well I can't be sure but mum's old boyfriend was a dealer and I remember that they got me to put his stuff in the loft as they were paranoid about getting raided. They kept going on about how it was over an ounce and it was about ten times smaller than what we've got. I reckon it must be about a kilo, which is like a thousand grams. That's a lot of cocaine."

Stacey stopped herself from saying that people killed for that amount as she didn't want to scare Lucia again. She felt sick to her stomach, her childhood had been ruined by her mother's drink and drug habit and the associates that came with it and now when she'd thought she'd finally got away from it all, she'd found herself in even more trouble.

"*Madonna me*. It's too much."

"I know. We need to give it back before the owners think we took it on purpose."

"We need to find that idiot Tomas. For sure he knows something. We don't have to mention the drugs; if he is involved I'm sure he will let us know."

"Maybe all of this is one big mistake."

"You think so?"

"How else would it end up in my bag? Maybe our bag got mistaken with another and it's just a simple case of handing it back and forgetting it ever happened. We might even get a reward! You're right, I think we should go to Space tonight and find Tomas.

"Hopefully he knows something and this will all be over!"

"I really hope so."

Stacey took Lucia's hand in her own, feeling empowered by her ability to pull it together. The feeling quickly evaporated when she spotted a group of men pointing and waving in their direction.

"Don't look now but I think we have some company."

Lucia followed Stacey's gaze and tutted.

"Them? They look like stupid Italian boys. Just ignore them."

Stacey inspected their scrawny bodies and fuzzy hair a bit closer, relieved to see that Lucia was right.

"God I am so on edge, for a moment..." Stacey paused. "Come on, let's get back to the room. We need to sort this shit out."

The hotel corridor was shrouded in darkness as Lucia and Stacey approached their room.

"Look!" Stacey whispered, pointing to their open door.

"What the fuck?" she whispered back, gripping onto Stacey's hand.

"It's OK, Luce. If they are inside, it's better that we explain, then they can take their stuff and fuck off. You stay here, don't move, OK." Stacey pulled her hand away and carefully started to tip toe towards the open door. She tried to reassure herself by thinking logically about the situation. *If* someone was waiting inside to attack them, then surely the door would be shut. She cautiously peered through the split in the doorframe; the room was dimly lit by a crack in the blind and as far as she could see it looked empty. She called for Lucia, pausing to listen for any movement inside the room but there was none.

Lucia came running to her side as Stacey locked the door behind them and switched on the light.

"What the fuck?"

Their room was a mess; all the drawers and cupboards had been left open and their possessions were sprawled across the floor.

"Fucking animals," Lucia said, her hand shaking as she held up a pillow that had been cut open. Stacey went to the panel praying that whoever had broken into their room had found what they were so desperately looking for.

"Did they find it?" Lucia asked, barely able to keep the cigarette still in her hands as she lit it.

Stacey's stomach dropped as she noticed the panel still intact. The whole thing didn't make any sense. *Why had they come when they were out? And if they hadn't found what they wanted, why didn't they wait till they came back?*

"No it's still here! Maybe we were just robbed?" Stacey suggested, although she knew she was being optimistic. "Check your money."

"They don't take anything!" Lucia said, pulling out a wad of euros from the purse inside her suitcase.

"Maybe they got distracted by our underwear?" Stacey said, gathering up Lucia's thongs from the bed.

"Sick, fucking *bastardos*. Who breaks into someone's apartment, just to mess with it?"

"For sure it is the owner. They must have been disturbed. They will come back, of this I am sure." Lucia's voice was muffled as she poked her face through the curtains.

"Is there anyone out there?"

"I can't see. They could be hiding though."

"Well we don't know for sure but still, I think we should get out of here as soon as possible."

"Maybe they come back and we give them the drugs and all of this will be over."

"I don't think it's going to be that simple. Look at what they did to our room and our stuff." Stacey shuddered as she thought of the pillows that had purposely knifed.

"Whoever has done this to our room is definitely unhinged and we don't want to be here when they come back. We've got to find somewhere else to stay, somewhere far away before they decide to return."

"You're so right, fuck. Let me try to think where we can go. OK, there is a place in Playa den Bossa my friend stayed at before. It's close to Space. Even if it's busy, there are a lot of hotels round there we can try," Lucia explained, the colour starting to return to her face.

"Sounds like a plan to me. Let's ring a cab from our room and check the fuck out."

"OK, I'll ring them, I know where to say."

"Don't tell the reception where we're going though. If the low lives who done this to our room are floating around, we don't want them overhearing where we are going and following us there."

"What do you think? I'm stupid?" Lucia snapped, her usually pristine hair frizzing at the sides and her face dripping with sweat.

"No, of course I don't, but we're both stressed out so I was just reminding you, that's all."

"Sorry me, OK? I just don't like this situation at all." Lucia started to dial reception as Stacey gathered their possessions off the floor. She took the beach bag with the cocaine in it and placed it inside her suitcase, praying that she wouldn't be searched on their way to Playa den Bossa.

"It's gonna be at reception in ten minutes," Lucia said, as she placed down the phone.

There was no time for neatness as they crammed the rest of their stuff into the suitcases. Stacey shut the door quietly behind them as Lucia wheeled their cases to the lift. She couldn't stop her foot from tapping on the ground as they waited for the lift to arrive at the reception. The doors opened revealing an empty lobby and Stacey hurried to the desk whilst Lucia kept a look out. The receptionist raised an eyebrow when Stacey informed her they were checking out but seeing as they had already paid agreed to let them check out insisting that she print off a receipt as verification. Before she could reach her computer, Lucia and Stacey were out of the doors and onto the street. Even the taxi driver tried to stop them as they lifted their own suitcases into the boot but he was too slow.

"*Estás bien?*"

"*Si, si. Evissa Town. Par favour,*" Lucia commanded as they rushed into the back of the car, locking the doors behind them. As the taxi passed the harbour, Stacey kept her eyes peeled on the road, watching for any cars that seemed to be following them.

"Thank fuck for that," she said in a hushed tone, taking Lucia's sweaty palm into her own as they passed a signpost for *Evissa Town.* She prayed to herself that their move would give them the sanctuary they needed, until they were able to return the drugs to their rightful owner, but she knew it was just wishful thinking. Their lives were in danger and as long as the drugs were in their hands there would be no escape from it all. .

The Old Town

1

Lucia's gaze had been fixed on the window the whole journey and her hands were clasped so tight around the handle of her bag, her knuckles had gone white. Stacey thought back to her reaction at the hotel, she was usually so brave and fearless yet she had turned into a complete and utter nervous wreck. Not that Stacey could blame her, even she'd felt like she was breaking down.

The taxi drove past Amnesia and Stacey suddenly remembered the photo shoot and opening party they were supposed to be attending tomorrow. *Would they still be able to do it?* she hoped so. She didn't want the drugs to mess everything up for them, as selfish as it sounded, tomorrow was her big opportunity to shine and she was sure that Jorge would not be handing out second chances.

Unfortunately, what they were dealing with now was a lot bigger than an opening night and if they didn't sort it out, it could bring about severe implications. As inconvenient as it was, returning the drugs to their rightful owner had to be their priority.

"*Donde quieres ir?*" the taxi driver called into the back.

Stacey watched anxiously as the taxi drove past a residential area littered with busy restaurants then turned to Lucia, whose face lightened a little in response.

"*El taxis Figueretas, par favour.*"

The driver pulled up to a taxi rank opposite a big hotel and switched off his meter.

"This one?" Stacey asked, looking up at the six storey building in front of them.

"Oh no! We want something more secure than this. Anyone could walk in there."

Stacey inspected the open entrance of the hotel; Lucia was right, they definitely needed something less open

"OK where then?" Stacey asked nervously, coiling her fingers around the handle of her suitcase.

"Come." Lucia strode towards the end of the road, her suitcase in one hand and a cigarette in the other.

Stacey followed Lucia as they crossed the road and headed to a smaller back street.

Some of the residents were smoking on the balconies that hung from the high rise buildings, their eyes scanning the girls as they walked past. Stacey caught a waft of garlic coming from the bar on the corner and as she looked towards it, the group of men who were gathered outside shouted out to them. Not appreciating the attention, Stacey averted her gaze to a painting of a semi-naked woman on the wall next to the bar. The Diamond Rose, was written on a sign above the ornate wooden door and there was a poster of a naked girl with only roses covering her modesty. The writing on the poster claimed that there were continuous shows all night with naked girls from around the world. Stacey couldn't help but wonder about the type of punters who frequented a place situated in the backstreets of Ibiza. Just past The Diamond Rose there was a small doorway with Hostelaria Ibiza written on the door in gold lettering.

"This is it," Lucia said, putting out her cigarette and pressing the buzzer.

The door clicked open in response, inside it smelt like coffee and cigarettes and Stacey could just make out a silhouette of a woman behind a frosted glass screen. Lucia rang the bell on the counter and the screen was prised open. Stacey instantly recognized the woman from the poster next door; although with her flawless skin, blue eyes, dark hair and naturally pouting lips she was much more beautiful in real life.

"*Ahola*?" Her voice was flat and her smile didn't reach her eyes as she addressed the girls.

Lucia talked to her in Spanish as Stacey tried her best to look like she understood what was being said.

"I have something for you both," she replied in English. "But I require a fifty euro deposit in advance as well as payment for all the nights you wish to stay. I do not tolerate partying, uninvited guests, or drugs." She looked into Stacey's eyes, her gaze cold and slightly intimidating.

Stacey tried her best to keep her composure as she thought about the big package of cocaine she had sitting in her suitcase.

"OK, no problem. We stay three nights."

Stacey was glad that Lucia was doing all the talking, she couldn't shake off the feeling that the woman could see right through her and that any effort that she made to speak would come out like a stuttering mess.

"The minimum stay is one week. It's eighty euros a night, so that works out five hundred and sixty euros. We accept visa or cash."

"I want to see the room first," Lucia demanded, the agitation evident in her voice.

"I'm afraid it's hotel policy that you pay first *then* we take you to your room. Believe me, this time in the season it won't be easy to find somewhere else, so take it or leave it."

Lucia turned to Stacey, her eyes conveying to her that although this woman was a bitch, they didn't have a lot of choice but to accept her conditions. Stacey nodded in encouragement, biting down on her lip as she did so.

"Yes we take," Lucia answered, her tone devoid of any of its usual pleasantries.

"OK, good. Are you paying card or cash?"

Stacey knew Lucia wanted to tell the woman where to go but defeated and desperate she reached into her bag. Taking the cue, Stacey pulled out the remaining five hundred euros from her purse and handed it to Lucia; she was now officially broke.

"Thank you, ladies," the woman said, almost smirking at them.

For a split second, Stacey feared the woman would do them over and was relieved when she saw her reach for a key from the rack behind her and indicate for them to follow her upstairs. Stacey and Lucia had to lift their suitcases up three flights of stairs and both of them were out of breath as they reached their room.

"OK there you are. Any problems, keep them to yourselves. I'm busy." The woman laughed, then changed her expression to deadly serious as she shut the door behind her.

"That woman is something else, no? Normally I would not give the bitch anything but we need this room. It's the only one I know that is completely safe from the outside, so at least no one can get to us."

"Yeah you know no one is coming past her!" Stacey said, comforting herself that the room was at least clean, fairly spacious and had two good sized single beds. She opened her suitcase and checked the package of cocaine was still intact.

"It's OK?"

"Yep it's fine. How far away are we from Space?"

"It's about ten minutes from here but we can get a taxi."

"Sounds like a plan."

"We gonna have to hide the drugs though, we don't wanna that the bitch finds it."

"Can you bloody imagine? She seems well dodgy. Did you see her picture on that strip club?"

"The one next door?"

"Yeah she must work there or something which is a bit weird. don't you think?"

"Yeah for sure we gonna have to hid the drugs well from her."

Stacey and Lucia spent the good part of an hour patting down the walls and cupboards. The whole place seemed impenetrable and they nearly gave up till Stacey managed to shift the panel from the outside of the bath.

"It's not completely secure but hopefully it will hold everything for now," she said, placing the bag under the bath. "We just got to remember to take it out when we shower."

"I pray it's OK there until we manage to find the owners."

"Or before they find us." Stacey turned to Lucia who had suddenly gone very pale.

"Sorry, Luce."

"It's OK, it's not your fault you're just speaking the truth. I just want this whole mess to be over; I can't bear the thought of what these men could do to us."

"Nothing is going to happen to us. All we have to do is find that Tomas guy, give the drugs back then we can get on with our time here. Eventually this will all be just a distant memory."

"I hope so, baby. I hope so."

The car park at Space was heaving with people as Stacey and Lucia pulled up in the taxi. The queue looked massive and Stacey started to doubt that they would even be able to get anywhere near the entrance. People were tutting as Lucia and she pushed their way to the front. Stacey scanned the area for Tomas and almost ducked when she spotted the security guard with the dragon tattoo from before.

"Don't look now Luce, but it's the security who took that guy's drugs." Stacey tried her best to shield her face without looking too obvious.

"We definitely don't wanna speak to him," Lucia whispered to her. "Let's find another one and ask where is Tomas."

"Him," Stacey said, spotting a lone security guard. With his shoulder length blond hair and the numerous bracelets that adorned his wrists, he appeared a lot more laid back compared to the other angry-looking guards

"Hello, excuse me." Stacey got the guard's attention and his face lighted up in response but as they walked towards him he straightened himself up and stood in a more authoritative manner.

"Is there a problem, ladies? You can't stand here," he commanded, his deep voice speaking with an accent Stacey couldn't place.

"We're here to see Tomas. Is he working tonight?"

"Tomas?" He seemed to relax at the mention of his colleague. "Wait here a second and I'll ask for you."

"I pray he gonna help us," Lucia said, grabbing onto Stacey as the guard walked off to find Tomas.

"Me too, me too." Stacey tried to calm herself but it was no use. Her nerves were shot to pieces at the thought of coming face-to-face with the man who had possibly planted them with a kilo of cocaine.

Ten minutes later, the blond security guard walked back, his face screwed up in confusion as he approached.

"Ladies I'm sorry, but I have bad news for you. Tomas didn't come to work today. He was due in tonight but didn't show up. It's very unlike him. Maybe he was too fucked up.

"You ladies OK? You look like you've seen a ghost. Are you good friends with him? Do you want me to pass on a message when he comes back to work?"

"He's not in? Are you sure? We really need to speak to him, it's pretty urgent."

"I'm sorry ladies but he hasn't been in. I asked everyone. Is there anything I can help you with?"

Stacey and Lucia exchanged a look as if to say *do we trust him?* Lucia shook her head and pulled out her phone.

"Do you have his number?" she asked the guard, who appeared uneasy at the request.

"I really shouldn't give you his number, but hey, I don't see what harm it can do. Wait a sec."

He pulled out his mobile and scrolled through his phone as Stacey waited, her whole body tight with the tension that was building up inside her.

"OK it's 3321884467. When you speak to him tell him to get his arse to work! Right I'm needed at the gates, I better go. Good luck."

"OK thanks for your help."

Lucia had already started dialling the number as the security stopped in his tracks and turned back towards them.

"One thing, ladies. I know that Tomas does security for Bora Bora. They have the opening party across the road tomorrow. Maybe he will have crawled out of his hole by then. Sorry I couldn't help you more."

"OK thanks, we really appreciate it," Stacey replied, her eyes focusing on Lucia whose ear was pressed against the receiver.

"OK well, hope to see you soon." He gave Stacey a flirty wink and walked back towards the gates.

"Something about that didn't sound right," Stacey said, concerned that Tomas was nowhere to be found. "Can you get hold of him?"

"I'm trying, wait. For sure he knows something. *Porca Troya!* It's not connecting."

Lucia's words echoed through Stacey, maybe it was just coincidental but things didn't seem right. She waved down a taxi, suddenly anxious that they were being watched.

"Come on, let's get back," Stacey said, feeling a chill come over her as they pulled away from Space. Somehow, the disappearance of Tomas and the discovery of the drugs was linked and Stacey wasn't looking forward to finding out how.

2

The sound of running water woke Stacey from her deep slumber. For a split second, she forgot all about the drugs and their room being raided. Then it hit her and she felt the sense of impending dread once again loom over her body. Lucia's bed was empty and by the sounds coming from the bathroom, showering. *Thank God she remembered to move it,* Stacey thought as she noticed the beach bag poking out from underneath Lucia's bed sheet. She peeled herself out of her bed and examined her face in the mirror. The dark circles from the day before had cleared a little and her brief exposure to the sun had caused her normally pale complexion to have a rosier glow. She ran through all the previous day's events in her mind. It didn't seem possible that so much had happened within three days of her arriving on the island. She tried to think about the things they could have done differently but there was nothing that struck her. It was obvious they needed to head to Bora Bora (whatever that was) today and try to find Tomas. Stacey opened the heavy silver lined curtains, and took in the view before her. It wasn't the postcard picture they'd had back in San Antonio, she could barely see past the white apartments she'd noticed from the night before. She craned her neck to the right and spotted a sandy beach in the distance. It looked so inviting, she was gutted that they had to go to this Bora Bora place today instead.

Lucia emerged from the shower, a flowery fragrance following her as she sat down on one of the chairs.

"Morning. You were up early. Did you sleep OK?"

"Not so good at the beginning but in the end, not so bad. You?" she replied, no longer sporting the strained expression she'd had from the day before.

"Well as soon as my head hit the pillow, I was out for the count, so yeah I slept really well considering how stressful yesterday was. It's a good job you remembered to take the coke out. I don't think we would have been able to give it back if it had all turned to paste."

Lucia smiled distractedly as she took off her towel revealing her bronzed and toned body underneath. *What I wouldn't give to look like that naked*, Stacey thought to herself as Lucia put on her gold bikini. "Are we going to the beach first?" Stacey asked, suddenly excited at the prospect.

"What do you mean? We are going to Bora Bora."

"Yes, but the beach before?"

"Baby, Bora Bora *is* the beach."

Stacey wasn't sure she would be able to enjoy any party with the drugs hanging over them but as they headed towards Playa den Bossa beach, next to groups of excitable people dressed in skimpy beachwear, she couldn't help but be influenced. A red marquee that signalled the entrance to Bora Bora was guarded by a bald security guard, who as they approached put his hand out to stop them.

"Open," he said in English, indicating Lucia's bag.

"I don't have anything," she protested, reluctantly handing over her bag.

Stacey quickly scanned the area for Tomas; inside the marquee there was a restaurant, a small bar and a screened DJ booth that faced a dance floor but no sign of the sweaty bandanna wearing guard. The whole place extended out onto a seemingly endless beach where hundreds of sunbeds, tables and umbrellas were all lined up on the sand. Even though it was only 11 a.m., house music was being played through the massive speakers and there were already some early revellers with sunglasses on, dancing with drinks in hand.

"I need to search it, otherwise you don't come in." Lucia huffed as the guard unzipped her bag.

"Is Tomas in today?" Stacey asked, as the man rummaged through Lucia's bag.

"Tomas? How do you know him?" he asked, looking up from his search.

"He knows our friend Mary."

"Aw, Mary the tall one from Australia he is always taking about."

"Yeah that's the one. Is he working today?"

"He is supposed to be but no one has seen him this morning. I know he likes to get a bit *loco* but not usually so early in the season." He laughed at his own joke and Stacey smiled back, trying to hide the panic that was growing inside of her. He handed back Lucia her bag and his face softened as he noticed Stacey's desolate expression. "When he comes in I can tell him to come see you?"

"Yes please if you don't mind."

"Of course I don't. How could I refuse two beautiful ladies?" He eyed up Lucia who turned away from him, steadying her eyes on the beach ahead.

"Thank you, we would appreciate that."

"That was so weird," Stacey said in a hushed tone, as they walked off. "Why hasn't he turned up to work again? There is definitely something dodgy going on."

"I know baby, it's so fucked up."

"God the food smells great. I'm starving can we get something to eat?" Stacey's asked her stomach was grumbling as she spotted a pizza being brought out from the kitchen.

"Oh, OK sure. Me not so much but yes we can eat first."

"Well if Tomas does decide to make an appearance, it will be a perfect place to spot him," Stacey said, pointing to the table closest to the entrance. "We can also try to ring him whilst we wait."

Lucia pulled out her phone and started to dial as Stacey looked over at a tattooed guy with his arms stretched out towards the sun as he danced.

"It's switched off. I really don't like this, baby."

"Maybe he's lost it. Or he's on a bender and not charged it?"

"I don't think so, it's way too coincidental. Look, order me a gin and tonic, I'm going to the *cac-ca*, OK?"

"What are you having to eat?"

"Anything, baby, you decide."

"OK well the toastie sounds good considering I'm broke,"

"OK get me one too," Lucia said, grabbing her bag and walking hurriedly towards the toilets.

The drinks arrived just as Lucia came back, her face looking less stressed than when she left.

"I've had an idea, baby!"

"Oh yeah. What's that?"

Lucia lit a cigarette and downed her drink.

"Woah, you were thirsty!"

Lucia was smiling behind her glasses as the white smoke from her cigarette billowed out in front of her.

"So what's this idea then?"

"As you know, tonight is the opening party at Amnesia and Nico will be there. I don't know why I didn't think of it sooner. He has so many contacts, for sure he will help us out. As much as I don't want to speak to him, I know he will do right by us."

"OK. It's definitely worth a try. Are you sure you can trust him though?"

"Yes of course. Anyway, what other choice do we have?"

Stacey let out a sigh; with Tomas doing a disappearing act and someone who was clearly deranged hot on their tail it was true, they didn't have many options.

"OK. So you think he'll be at Amnesia tonight?"

"For sure. He never misses the opening party."

There was a pause in conversation as both Lucia and Stacey contemplated their next move.

"You want to get a bed with me? We can relax on the beach for a little?"

Stacey really wanted to go and chill somewhere quiet till the opening tonight but she could tell by Lucia's toe tapping that she wanted to stay and after all they'd been through she knew they needed some sort of relief from the stress. Plus, the beach did look inviting and despite herself she was enjoying the music that was being played. She followed Lucia to the beds in front of the sea and watched from behind her glasses as almost every male, and even some of the females, checked Lucia out. Not that she could blame them, with her white denim hot pants and gold bikini top Lucia looked like someone straight out of a magazine. A long haired man walked over to them and Lucia negotiated a couple of sunbeds. Stacey tried to give her the remainder of her money over to Lucia but she pushed her away dismissively.

"Shh. It's my treat, OK. Now we have fun!"

Within minutes, the long haired man walked back over with an ice-cold jug of Sangria with freshly cut oranges and strawberries bobbing at the top.

"Here you are. Enjoy, bitchy!"

"I can't afford all this, Lucia. I'm practically broke. What with the room change and stuff."

"It's OK really, I look after you. We've had so much stress let's try to enjoy," Lucia smiled as she poured them a glass. "To having a good time, no matter what!" Lucia toasted, raising her glass towards Stacey.

"To having a good time," Stacey replied, trying to forget about the kilo of cocaine that was sat inside the bath panel of their room.

"Baby, I'm going to the toilet. You be OK here, No?"

"Yeah I'll be fine," Stacey replied as she surveyed the groups of people who had started to turn up. No one appeared to be acting suspiciously and Stacey noticed how fashionably everyone was dressed. Back in England, Lucia had made her purchase a pair of denim shorts and a white bikini and as she looked at all the other girls who were dressed in bright bikinis, some even wearing jewellery, she was glad she'd taken her advice. Her skin was devoid of any make-up and normally she would be in panic mode because her millions of freckles were on display but today she didn't care. She put all her insecurities to the back of her mind and focused on the gorgeous beach in front of her. She could feel the heat of the sun boring down onto her and it lifted her up inside. Feeling brave, she took her phone out of her shoulder bag and switched it on. She hadn't dared to do it since leaving England, too scared that her mother's pleading phone calls would send her over the edge and make her abandon her life in Ibiza but there was nothing, not even a text. *She must be on one of her benders,* she thought to herself, relieved. Despite the trouble Lucia and herself were in, at least she knew she'd done the right thing leaving home. Stacey put her sunglasses on (another purchase with the help of Lucia) and sipped on her sangria whilst she watched the tanned and muscular men in front of her play volley ball. She'd never seen so many good-looking men in one place and she found her thoughts wandering to the mysterious guy at Space. She was an idiot not to ask for his number, not that she would have even been able to write it down, the state she was in. From the corner of her eye, she noticed someone staring at her. She adjusted her vision without moving her head so she could get a better look. His hair was shaved close to his head and he was sporting dark Ray Ban glasses. With his white skin and skinny arms, he stood out from the rest of the men on the beach. She tried to act like she hadn't noticed him and pretended to write something on her phone but there was no mistaking that he was watching her. His whole body was turned directly towards her. She tried to not panic and forced herself to look at the men in front. *Was she imagining it all?* She glanced back at him, her heartbeat quickened as she saw him still sitting in the same position. This time he seemed to notice her, reaching for his camera he aimed it to the sky as if to take a picture. Stacey wanted to confront him, *maybe he would know something about the drugs?* With his serious expression, she doubted he would welcome any type of questioning.

"So I was in the toilet when this bitch stood on my toes. You know I had to push the stupid cow. I don't know how she can go through her life being like an elephant. The music is *fantastico* no? I love Bora, Bora." Lucia stood in front of Stacey, blocking her view of the guy in front.

"What happened? Why do you look like this?"

"Don't look now but there's this guy who's been watching me."

"Why of course he is watching you, eh? In your bikini, this is men. I bet he's Italian."

"Show me the little pervert."

Stacey searched for him on the beach but the spot where he had been sitting was empty.

"He's gone."

"What? Are you sure?"

"I'm serious. One moment he was there staring at me, then he just disappeared."

"Baby it's nothing, you are just anxious. You need to relax. Have some more sangria, OK?"

"I'm positive he was looking at me and not in a pervy way, Luce. Call me paranoid but he could be the one who did over our room. There was something dodgy looking about him."

"Dodgy? You can tell that by just looking? Come on? He is looking at you because you are beautiful. How many times do I have to tell you this, *principessa*?" Lucia was dancing as she spoke as if she didn't have a care in the world.

Stacey felt like she was caught up in some crazy parallel universe where it didn't matter if someone was following you, or whether your bag had been filled with drugs by a man who had gone missing, the music still played as loud as possible and the people surrounding still danced and got high. It was total madness and unfortunately, Stacey had found herself slap bang in the middle of it all.

A handful of partygoers had already started dancing on the tables by the time Stacey managed to drag Lucia out of Bora Bora. The photo shoot at Amnesia started at seven, the parade at ten and the grand opening afterwards, so when it hit half-five Stacey knew they needed to go back to the apartment as soon as possible to prepare. They headed out of the marquee and Stacey checked again with the security guard at the door but there had still been no sign of Tomas. Stacey pulled Lucia's bag across her shoulder, and winced. Her skin felt tender and suddenly she realised why. With everything that had been going on, she'd forgotten to re-apply her sun cream. She looked down at her body with nervous trepidation, her skin was a little pinker on her knees and feet but luckily the rest of her was just lightly tanned. She breathed a sigh of relief, as long as the pink didn't turn red, she might be OK, if not, she would definitely be sporting the 'lobster look' at the opening tonight. Even though they'd only had two jugs of sangria, Lucia seemed completely out of it. Stacey had to physically drag her away from Bora Bora whilst she was still dancing but she couldn't be mad. Bora Bora was the type of place that you never wanted to leave.

It was the first party she'd been to on a beach and if she hadn't caught the weird man watching her, she would have really enjoyed it. Instead she'd spent the whole day looking out for him and an increasingly inebriated Lucia. They got into the taxi and Stacey checked for him again, it was more crowded on the street than before but she swore she saw a glimpse of a pale man in dark glasses leant by the wall near the supermarket across the road. She stopped breathing, feeling almost winded at the implications of the sighting.

Was he waiting for them? Before she could get a proper look, the taxi pulled away.

"*Bonita*! Are you OK? Did you enjoy Bora Bora? *Bonita*?" Lucia asked Stacey, who was engulfed in her thoughts.

"It's him."

"Who?"

"The guy from the beach, I saw him. He was watching us get in the taxi!"

"Baby, you are being paranoid! No one is watching us."

"You know someone could be and maybe you would notice if you weren't trying to have such a good time all the time."

"What? That's not fair. We moved the apartment and no one followed us, we both saw.

"So, we are safe? You must calm yourself. Tonight, I will find Nico, he will help us, OK?

"Please for now don't worry. Try to enjoy yourself. Remember what you leave behind. No more misery. You deserve to be happy."

Stacey thought about all the times she'd cried about the injustice of her life and how Ibiza had been a beacon for her new life and happiness.

"OK, I know. We still have to be careful though. There is someone out there looking for us. We can't pretend it's not happening but you're right, I've been waiting for tonight for a long time. I'm not going to let anything ruin it."

"Yes that's better. You are going to love the opening party, it's like nothing you ever experience."

Stacey smiled as she thought of the two amazing parties she'd been to so far.

"I really can't wait, Luce. Thanks for sorting my head out. I'm just finding it hard to not worry over something or another, I've been doing it all my life."

"Shh! It's normal. Now, let's get ready to party! Woo!"

Stacey couldn't help but check one last time as they let themselves into the Hostelaria. There was nobody there and Stacey hoped that she'd just imagined it all. The moody receptionist from before was behind her desk and smiled as they walked in.

"*Ahola Chicas*. You been to Bora Bora?"

Stacey looked at Lucia who was completely oblivious to the woman's sudden change in attitude.

"Yes, we had an amazing time. The music was *Molto Bello*, and the men soo handsome!" Lucia exclaimed, as she started dancing in the reception area.

"Come on, Luce, I've got to get you ready. No offence but I think I'm going to need a bit more make-up than usual!"

"You staying on the island for long? You have a lot of stuff."

"We stay here the whole summer, so if you treat us OK and we will stay here a long time." Lucia was slurring her words as she spoke.

"And what is it that you do? If you don't mind me asking?" the woman asked, showing no signs that she'd noticed Lucia was drunk.

"I am a dancer at Amnesia and my friend is an amazing make-up artist. Is OK for you?"

The woman let out a small smile; looking down at her manicured fingernail she changed the tone of her voice, as if she was speaking to a small child.

"I don't imagine it pays very well. Have you seen the club next door?"

"The *bordello*?" Lucia asked, her face animated with disgust.

"It's not a *bordello*, thank you, but a very exclusive hostess club. My name is Summer, I am the owner. I am always looking for pretty girls to work there. You can make endless money plus your accommodation can be reduced by fifty percent."

"I am a professional dancer. I would never dream to do that. Thanks but no thanks."

Summer smiled at Lucia's response yet her eyes remained cold. Stacey knew that Lucia had offended her but she couldn't blame her for how she had reacted, the place was as seedy looking as they came.

"No problem ladies. Just remember *Evissa* isn't as easy as you think. Sometimes it's better to have a life where money is no problem, where you don't have to work hard for a few euros, where you can buy the things you like. Think about it. If you change your mind, you know where I am."

"We won't, *believe me!* Come on, Stacey." Stacey was glad that Summer had finally killed Lucia's party bubble even if there was something really unnerving about the way her eyes bored into them as they walked up the stairs.

3

All of Stacey's previous worries were left at the door as she and Lucia walked through the caverned entrance to Amnesia. The huge club was so empty, it echoed their footsteps back to them as they made their way across the dance floor. Stacey couldn't help but smile to herself as she imagined all the thrill seekers who would walk through the doors that night. It was going to be one hell of a party by Lucia's accounts and Stacey was so glad she would get to be a part of it.

"Lucia! *Amore meo! Comi stai?*" Lucia kissed the guy who appeared in front of them twice on the cheeks.

"*Ciao amore! Benne graze! Tu? Allora, me amica,* Stacey. My make-up artist and best friend."

"*Benne Lucia. Ciao Bella! Piacerie,* Francesco," he exclaimed as he kissed Stacey.

"Hi, nice to meet you, Stacey."

"You are English?"

"Yes."

"Wow, so *bella*!"

Stacey found herself blushing at Francesco's compliment. He had piercing blue eyes that made her feel undressed in one glance and was wearing an open waistcoat that showed off his well-chiselled six pack. She couldn't help but swoon a little in his presence.

Francesco continued to speak to Lucia in Italian and even though Stacey didn't have a clue what they were talking about she found herself completely mesmerized by their animated hand gestures.

"Oh sorry me. My English is not so good. I don't mean to be offence," Francesco said, his face full of concern.

"No problem! My Italian is non-existent; so don't feel you have to speak in English for me."

"She is so cute, no?" Francesco said, smiling at Stacey with his brilliant white teeth. "Yes, baby! She is my best friend from London. I love this bitchy!" Lucia placed her arm around Stacey.

"You go upstairs *Bellas*?"

"Yes we go. See you there?"

"Of course. *Ciao Bellas*!"

"*Ciao Bello*!"

"*Ciao*," Stacey said, using her newly found Italian word. "Cor, he's gorgeous."

"You like Francesco eh? He is beautiful, no?"

"He sure is. Is he, you know, gay?" Stacey asked, wondering if, like the theatre they worked at back in London, most of the male dancers were gay.

"No baby! He is just Italian, it's normal for the men to be more passionate than the women. They take longer to get ready than us and probably cry more too! You want that I talk to Francesco for you? I think he liked you."

"Oh no! But wow, do you think he does? That's ridiculous! He is so beautiful but not my type at all. I like more rugged, masculine men."

"Like that guy from Space?"

"No! Well yeah, I mean how did you know?"

"I could see that you like him even though you were fucked up!"

"Was it that obvious?"

"No! Of course not!" Lucia giggled and poked Stacey in the ribs.

"So I was obvious? Cringe! Oh well, it doesn't matter now I'll never see him again."

"He liked you I could see."

"You think everyone likes me!"

"Well they do! And why not? You are amazing! It is natural."

"You do make me laugh!" Stacey said as she screwed up her face and looked away.

"As for my mysterious rescuer. If he liked me so much, he would have asked for my number. Instead he just left me disabled on the sofa."

"Haha, baby, you were soo disabled!"

"Yeah thanks! Actually better that I don't see him now."

"Ibiza always has a way of bringing people together, it's a magnetic island. I have a strong feeling you will meet again."

"Really?" Stacey said, letting out a deep sigh.

"I know so! My *bella regazza.*"

Stacey had to laugh, since they'd left the apartment Lucia had started to sober up and was starting to sound like her old self.

"How you feeling about seeing Nico again?"

"Not really happy to be honest. He is such a *bastardo*! But I know he can help with our situation. He knows people. Maybe he can't be trusted when it comes to love but he is a good man. That was the reason I found it hard to let him go."

Stacey saw a sadness in Lucia's face. Nico had ended their relationship suddenly and she knew it had broken Lucia's heart.

"Come on, bitchy! Let's go upstairs, Jorge will be waiting for us and you have all the dancers to meet!"

Stacey followed Lucia to the top of the club, trying to take in the layout but it was no use, the club was like a massive dark labyrinth.

"That's where I dance," Lucia said, pointing to a narrow platform directly above the dance floor.

"Jesus," Stacey said, realizing that the platform was at least fifteen foot off the ground.

"This way," Lucia said, beckoning her to a hidden door.

No one noticed Lucia and Stacey as they stepped out onto the roof top area. Being so high up you could see out for miles into the distance and Stacey stood there for a second, marvelling at the full moon which illuminated the villas nestled in the mountainous landscape below. There had to be over sixty people milling around them, all of whom seemed to be busy doing something. There were bulbed mirrors across one side of the wall, a row of lockers, and numerous crates of water scattered around. Beautiful women, all in various stages of undress, were conversing with each other in languages Stacey had never heard before. They all seemed so carefree as they stood in front of each other half naked. It was in stark contrast to the theatre back home where the stars had their own dressing rooms and during intervals they would constantly boast about their latest parts or royal encounters. Everything was a lot more open here and everyone seemed so much more cool and relaxed.

"Stacey. Come here." Jorge's voice boomed above all the chatter. He was wearing loose black cotton trousers and a black vest top, his curly hair hung loosely by his waist.

"Stacey, this is Carmen." Jorge walked her over to a woman applying glittery lipstick onto a dancer's pouting lips. Stacey waited for her to introduce herself but she didn't look up from her work.

"Hi Carmen, it's good to meet you. I'm Stacey, I'm here to help you."

"I don't need any help," she said, her voice curling as she turned back to her make-up.

Jorge put his hand on Stacey's shoulder and whispered in her ear.

"Don't let her upset you. She is a fiery woman who would never admit that she needs help but as you can see, we have a lot of girls and guys who need your help tonight. I need the girls looking fresh for the shoot, no imperfections on display. Which will be a challenge considering most of them are still recovering from Space's opening party."

"No problem," she said, grateful she'd paid attention in class to the airbrush technique which really did hid a multitude of sins..

"Where is Lucia?" Jorge asked, his eyes searching around the room.

"I'm not sure, probably in the toilet or something."

"OK. Well I can trust you to get on then. The photo shoot will be taking place in less than an hour. If you set yourself up over there, I will send the girls over to you."

Stacey nodded, surveying the area that was allocated to her.

"Lucia says you have talent. Don't prove her wrong. No mess-ups and no screw ups. You got me?" There was an unmistakably threatening tone to his voice and Stacey nearly stammered as she answered him back.

"No problem. I won't let you down." She reassured him as she grabbed her case and started to set herself up.

Carmen looked like she was having some sort of altercation with Jorge and Stacey hoped she would soften to the idea of her working there but she wasn't going to hold her breath. There was still no sign of Lucia but she couldn't go searching, Jorge was already pointing a girl with long blonde hair in her direction. She was dressed in a stringy bikini and sat herself down on the chair in front of Stacey, without saying a word.

"Hi there," Stacey said, but the girl simply grunted at her and pulled her phone out. Stacey tried not to let it dishearten her, maybe she'd had a long night but she guessed it was probably because she was friends with Carmen.

Once finished, Stacey stood back and admired her work. Even though the blonde girl was naturally very beautiful, Stacey was pleased that the make-up she had applied had made her look even more stunning. The whole time the girl had remained poker-faced but as she examined herself in the mirror for the first time, her face broke out into a smile.

"Cool! You are actually good! Thank you!" With that she rejoined the other girls as they cooed over her appearance. Soon a queue of girls stood in front of Stacey, asking her to 'transform' them like she had done the first girl.

"Your freckles are so beautiful, Stacey. You are far too gorgeous to be the make-up artist. You should be dancing with us." Her third client, Carolina from Brazil, hadn't stopped talking since she'd sat down on the chair, which was making it difficult for Stacey to do her make-up. Not that she minded that much, Carolina was so friendly and charming, Stacey found herself listening intently to her stories. She was blown away by how Carolina had managed to escape her poverty-stricken life in Rio De Janeiro to follow her dream of becoming a dancer. It reminded her of her own journey – not that she mentioned it – she'd put her past behind her now and that's where she wanted it to stay.

When the subject came round to Lucia's and her friendship, Stacey found herself searching around the room for her. She was really starting to get worried now; after all, she was the star of the show and the reason why she was there. *She couldn't just go missing for ages, could she?*

"Oh yes, Lucia, our ballerina, have you seen the way her body is moving? Something special she is. When she dances to Sven Vath, it's like the whole club follows her."

Just on cue, Stacey spotted Lucia coming through the door with Francesco. They made sure the coast was clear before separating off into the changing rooms. Lucia's eyes met Stacey's from across the room and for a brief moment she saw a look of pure panic on her face. She watched as Lucia quickly managed to exchange it for a more carefree expression as she came sauntering over to Stacey, her eyes focusing in on Carolina's face.

"This is incredible, baby. I knew you'd be brilliant!" she exclaimed, her eyes not meeting Stacey's.

"Thanks, Luce. Where have you been? I've been looking for you."

"Oh just warming up before the shoot." She glanced at Stacey for a brief second before picking up a make-up brush.

"*Ahola* Lucia, *Comi stais*?" Carolina asked, breaking the tension.

"*Benne graze, tu*?" Stacey noticed that Lucia was talking a lot faster than normal as she conversed in Italian with Carolina, and that the eye make-up she had applied was now smudged into rings around her wide eyes.

"Close please," Stacey instructed as she sprayed the finishing spray across Carolina's face. "OK, you're done."

"Oh that is *so* beautiful. Thank you so much." Carolina air kissed Stacey twice.

"Come find me later, OK?"

"OK, cool I will," Stacey said distractedly, her mind preoccupied with Lucia's disappearance and her strange behaviour.

"Your make-up is literally smudged all around your eyes, Lucia. Is everything OK?" she asked, trying to keep her tone as neutral as possible.

Lucia nodded as she stared into the mirror and tried to rub underneath her eyes using her fingers.

"It's going to take more than that. Here sit down." Lucia sat down; her body stiffened as Stacey came towards her.

"Where were you, babe? I was looking for you."

"What do you mean? Oh, Francesco? He is just a friend."

"No not that. I mean you, you've been acting strange all day. Don't take this the wrong way but are you high?"

"Are you serious?" Lucia asked as she started to push herself up off the chair.

"Lucia sit down. Everyone will be looking, please." Lucia huffed and sat back down.

"What are you saying to me? You think I am on drugs?"

"I'm sorry. It's just you seem a bit on edge. Are you OK?"

"Of course I am not high! Maybe I am a little worried for the, well you know, but high? Are you serious?"

"OK, just forget I said anything."

"I'm sorry if I left you but you did fine, no? Don't worry for me. There are no problems. We all have a show to put on and I am preparing for this. This is my area, I know what I'm doing so no panicking, OK?"

Stacey wiped the rings from underneath Lucia's eyes and wiped her brush.

"OK. You're right, this is your area. If you want to talk about anything I'm here."

Stacey could tell by her reaction it was best to drop the subject especially as she didn't have any concrete proof.

"Am I finished?" Lucia asked shortly.

"Yes you're finished," Stacey replied in her best peace-making tone. Without saying a word, Lucia got up and marched across the room to where Francesco was. Taking his hand, she led him downstairs whilst Stacey looked on in shock.

For the next half hour, Stacey concentrated on her make-up as she tried to forget the altercation between Lucia and herself. The photographers arrived and the dancers started to organize themselves into groups for the shoot. Lucia had reappeared just in time and Stacey watched her from a distance as she kept adjusting herself in the mirror. The dancers were called out to the podium ledge and Stacey was beckoned to the tunnel at the back of the changing room. It led to a space behind the DJ box where you could clearly see the ledge in which the dancers performed. Everyone was lined up and Stacey spotted Lucia; the photographer leant down to the side of her, trying to catch her best angle as she contorted her body into position. Even though she'd acted nervous before she seemed full of confidence now and Stacey could tell her photos would come out good. She suddenly felt stupid for doubting her friend, maybe she was telling the truth and Stacey was just paranoid because of her mum's behaviour in the past.

"I need to talk to you, Stacey." She turned to see Jorge standing behind her, his face serious.

"Yes, OK go ahead."

"I just wanted to say thanks to you, you have done a very good job with the girls' make-up. Lucia was good to her word for once, you *are* talented."

"The girls are beautiful so they were easy to work, you don't have to thank me."

"You are too modest, as I said before most of the girls are recovering from the opening parties so I know it wasn't easy to make them look fresh. Talking of which, is Lucia OK?"

"Yeah of course, I think. Why's that?" Stacey said, trying to sound as genuine as possible.

"I'm not sure but I think she might be on something. I hope to God I'm wrong."

Jorge pointed to his nose as Stacey screwed up her face trying to hide her reaction.

"I think she is just under a lot of strain. She has been complaining of a stomach ache since we got some dodgy *Tapas* last night. Think she might have some sort of food poisoning and mixed with the big opening, I think it's all taking its toll."

"You're a good friend, covering for her. It's just Lucia isn't as strong as you think, the last time she started doing that stuff, she didn't sleep for four days. I'm afraid she is one of those people who just doesn't know when to say no. So if you know for sure, you have to try to get her to stop. It's no good for her, or the club so we both need her to stay clean otherwise everything gets fucked, OK?"

"OK, no problem. I'm sure everything is fine."

Stacey couldn't get Jorge' s words out of her head. *Lucia had a drug problem?* It was news to her, back home she'd seen her have a drink after work but that was all. She knew Lucia liked to indulge a little when she was in Ibiza but she'd never mentioned how out of control she could get. Stacey really wanted to confront Lucia over this new information but she knew it was pointless. Trying to change a person's view point, especially when they were high never went down well and if Lucia and she were going to get through the night they were going to have to stick together.

4

"Babe, come on, we've got to go. The bus has stopped." Lucia was slumped against the seat of the bus as four of the dancers clambered over her.

"Is she OK?" Ingrid, the German girl whose make-up Stacey had done, asked.

"I hope so. Lucia, come on, you've got to wake up!"

"*Catso Voi?*" she moaned, pushing Stacey back onto the seat as the other dancers looked on with horror. Opening her eyes, she stared at Stacey, her face scrunched up in confusion.

"Where are we?"

"We're in Ibiza Town, I think. We've got to meet Jorge. Do you need me to help you up?"

"Oh, OK. Yes, help me up, please."

"Do you want to go back to the apartment, babe? If you're not feeling well maybe it's better that you rest up?"

"No! It's fine, really."

Stacey was glad that Lucia didn't want to go home, if they both left Jorge in the lurch it would probably mean they wouldn't have a job to come back to. Not that it gave her much comfort, the state Lucia was in she wasn't sure if she would even make it through the parade, let alone the whole night.

"I'm going to try and get us some food and maybe a coffee, if you're up for it?"

"Eugh no. I'm OK, baby."

Stacey pulled Lucia up and helped her off the bus.

"You've got to eat something, babe. It will help to sober you up."

"OK, OK, stop. I am a professional I know what I'm doing."

"Yes, I know but you've drunk a lot."

"Stacey, stop to go on please. Follow me, I take us to Jorge."

Lucia held out her hand and led Stacey through the cobbled streets of Ibiza Town.

Stacey was mesmerized by the late night market stalls situated between small alcoves, the vine-entwined balconies and caverned bars, Ibiza Town was like going back in time.

House music was being played quietly from most bars but unlike San Antonio, where it was played as loud as possible, each sound had its own appreciation, no one was trying to outdo each other. The tourists visiting this area weren't at all like the beer swigging yobs you got along the West End, most were seated at candle-lit tables with champagne or wine bottles and the remains of what looked like beautiful dinners, their faces happy and carefree.

"Mm, can you smell that?" The smell was a magnificent mixture of baked dough, tomatoes, garlic and basil.

"That's El Pirata, they do amazing pizza," Lucia said, her eyes focused on the bar ahead of them.

"Let's go inside, *please.* I'm bloody starving!"

"You are always hungry, baby! I can't go in there, really. I need to sit down, see the bar over there?"

"Yeah," Stacey said, sighing.

"That's where we all wait. I can meet you there if you like."

"Oh yeah please. Do you want some pizza?"

"No really, I'm OK."

"OK," Stacey said, shrugging her shoulders, deciding she would buy Lucia a slice anyway.

Jorge was seated on a table outside the Amnesia bar; surrounded by all the dancers in their skimpy outfits, he looked like a proud lion with his pack. He made eye contact with Stacey and nodded in her direction. His eyes deliberately scanned the area behind her, as if to look for Lucia. Stacey looked around for her but once again she was nowhere to be seen. The hot pizza was starting to burn her hands so she ate her slice and placed Lucia's on the table, covering it with the napkin given. She spotted Francesco in the back of the crowd talking to a dark haired girl, his hands moving up and down her body as he smiled at her with his gleaming white teeth.

"Hey Francesco, have you seen Lucia? She said she was gonna wait for me here."

"Oh Lucia! Yes, she is so *loco* tonight. I try to help her, but she pushed me away. She's gone to the toilet with Petra, to try to sober up, if you know what I mean."

"*Yeah,* where did she get that stuff? It's amazing, so pure."

Francesco elbowed the girl in front of him not too subtly and she stopped talking. Stacey wanted to stay put and ask more but she knew it was now imperative that she find Lucia.

"She's in the toilets in the bar next door, my love, good luck."

"Thanks," Stacey said, shuffling past Jorge and into the next bar. There was a small queue formed outside the women's toilet and Stacey pushed her way to the front.

"I know you're in there, Lucia! Let me in or I'm going to pack my bags and go. I've had enough!"

The women in the queue looked at her like she was crazy but she didn't care. She pounded on the door till eventually it swung open. She was shocked when she saw Lucia almost collapsed against the sink, a note in one hand and a drink in the other.

"Baby, I'm sorry," Lucia said, her face looking like she was about to cry.

"Shut the door will you!" Petra the long haired girl from before shouted, as she knelt in front the toilet, the note still in her nose. Stacey was taken aback by the sheer audacity of the girl yet reluctantly she shut the door.

"I don't know who you think you are talking to me like that, but you need to get out of here right now, this is between Lucia and myself." Stacey could feel the blood rushing to her cheeks as Petra stared vacantly back at her.

"Lucia! You need to calm your friend down. We are in Ibiza, stop being such a bore!"

Stacey felt ready to blow but taking a deep breath, she managed to compose herself.

"If you don't get out now, I will tell Jorge exactly what you are both up to. Do you think he will appreciate you doing lines with her when she is already like this?"

Petra's pupils were all big like a Disney character as she turned to Lucia, whose head was swaying to some unknown tune.

"Leave!" Stacey shouted, letting all the anger come out.

Petra grabbed her bag and let herself out of the door.

"I know you're using that stuff, Lucia. I just don't get why you couldn't have told me? Last time I checked we didn't lie to each other so why have you acted like this? All the lying and sneaking behind my back, don't you think I had enough of it with my bloody mother?"

Lucia turned away from Stacey; her whole body seem deflated by Stacey's words.

"That's exactly why I didn't tell you, baby. You've had so much to deal with, I know you have to be sensible and strong. But I am not so strong. This whole situation really messed with my psychology. So I took a little from the bag, I'm sorry but I needed some strength for the opening night."

"But you don't need it, Lucia, you just think you do."

"Maybe you don't but today I did. I don't know how to stay cool and calm like you."

"So you thought that taking the drugs we are supposed to be giving back, would make things better?"

"I know it was stupid, but I just wanted to feel good again. I've been so fucked up, I just thought a little line and a drink would help, but I know it has got out of control."

Tears started to roll down Lucia's face as she spoke and it took all Stacey's resistance not to rush over to her and hug her.

"You can't just get fucked and think it's all going to be alright. If anything, it's going to make you feel worse. How much did you take?"

"I don't know, maybe five grams."

"Fuck's sake, Luce!"

"It was hard to break off!"

"You should have spoken to me about it."

"I knew you'd be pissed off."

"I'm more pissed off that you lied to me in the first place."

"Sorry me. I was just stressed and I wanted to have a good time."

"Jorge knows you're high, Luce. He warned me to keep an eye on you."

"What? Oh shit. What am I gonna do? I don't think I can dance. I can't even walk properly."

"Yes you can, Luce. You mustn't think like that. I've got some pizza for you outside."

"We can eat and sober up and you will be fine again, *trust me*. Come on we better go before Jorge comes to find us, remember you are the star and that I, and the club, need you tonight. Now give me what you've got left and we can put this all behind us and move on."

"No, I can't. If I stop now I won't dance. I need it just to keep me going."

"Are you insane? Come on, stop being an idiot, have some pizza and a coffee and sober the fuck up!"

"I know what you are saying makes sense, but I have gone too far. I promise after this no more cocaine, OK?"

Stacey let out a frustrated sigh.

"There is no telling you, is there? Well you know what? I'm not going to be part of this. On top of everything, you are putting our lives in danger, is there no end to your selfishness?"

"Stacey, try to stay calm. They are not going to notice a little bit, and even if they do, I'm sure they don't mind us taking a little for ourselves considering we have looked after it for them. We never asked for this situation, so we mustn't let it ruin our fun. Remember that we are in Ibiza baby, we have to try enjoy ourselves!"

Stacey watched in disbelief, as Lucia crouched down by the toilet seat. She unfolded a magazine page in her hand and opened it up to reveal a giant white rock of cocaine with white crumbs at the base of it. Tipping some out onto the toilet seat she started to rack up two lines.

"Are you fucking serious?"

"Yes, bitchy." A smile crept across her face as she looked at Stacey. "You worry way too much. Come, join in."

"I don't want one," Stacey said, crossing her arms. "And you should stop, you're already in a right state, you don't need any more."

"What's wrong with you? You take everything so serious. Just because you have one line doesn't mean you end up like your *mamma*."

"I'm not bloody stupid, Luce, of course I know I won't end up like my mum after one line. It's just not good if both of us are off our heads. What would Jorge say then?"

"Don't you think Jorge gets fucked up too? Everyone in Ibiza does. I know you wanna stay sensible but we have both had this horrible stress and I know for sure this will make you feel better. I don't wanna push you but you must try to relax and enjoy, this is Ibiza."

Stacey didn't know what came over her, maybe she was tired of saying no and doing the right thing, but as she stared at the cocaine before her she couldn't stop the expression, *if you can't beat them join them,* from entering her thoughts.

"*Alright.* I give in. I'll have a small one but after tonight, no more, OK?" She saw a devilish smile form across Lucia's lips and found herself nervously laughing. She leant over and sniffed the line Lucia had prepared for her. The bitter powder hit the back of her throat and instantly she felt a surge of adrenalin. Suddenly all the things she had been worrying about started to disappear. She felt empowered and ready to conquer whatever the night threw at her. Lucia did her line but was still struggling to get back up, so Stacey helped her on her feet; taking her hand she unlocked the door and led Lucia through the bar. They walked outside just in time to join the parade; tightening her grip on Lucia, Stacey led her down the cobbled pathway and towards the front of the group.

"You've got to try to stand up on your own, babe. It's looking well dodgy me holding you up like this."

Lucia's eyes widened and she grasped Stacey's arm even harder.

"Don't let go of me, Stacey; my legs have gone strange. I think I've got a cramp. If you don't help me to walk, Jorge will see that I am fucked up. Please, stay with me."

With no other choice, Stacey let Lucia use her as a crutch as the group marched through the cobbled streets of the Old Town. Stacey did her best to stay straight and not make it look like Lucia was relying on her for all her balance, but when she caught Jorge looking at them, his eyes revealing to her that he was fully aware of the situation, she knew there would be some sort of retribution. People lined up in the bars and streets to cheer them on as they walked past, and despite Lucia hanging onto her for dear life, Stacey actually started to enjoy herself. She even joined Lucia for her 'toilet stops' and the free shots at the bar. By the end of the parade, she was feeling quite high and a little drunk. *So what if she had lost a little control?* This was Ibiza, the craziest place she'd ever been to and she was sure that loosening the grip on her, usually, militant self-control wouldn't mean the end of the world.

5

Lasers danced across the crowd and onto Stacey's face as she negotiated her way through the heaving dance floor of Amnesia. The music was so loud; it felt like all of her other senses had been muted. She could just make out Jorge standing next to the bouncers at the bottom of the stairs. The upstairs area was now closed off and the rope that marked the entrance was being held open to let the dancers through. Some of the clubbers had stopped what they were doing to cheer the girls as they walked past. Stacey watched as the two English girls, who earlier had confessed to having taken an ecstasy tablet, stumbled up the stairs. Jorge had made it clear that he ran a professional set up, but most of the girls, including herself, had indulged and Stacey knew she would be needing a lot of make-up to make them appear fresh again. She watched as the people around her surrendered themselves to the music wishing that she too, could get lost inside the rhythm and momentarily forget all her responsibilities.

Jorge, as if sensing her desire for abandonment, called her towards him. Taking a deep breath, Stacey guided a still fragile Lucia up the stairs, and towards the changing rooms. The music wasn't as loud in the changing rooms and Stacey managed to pull herself together without too much effort. A queue instantly formed in front of her, with girls wanting their look made more 'dramatic' for the stage. She worked as fast as she could and was relieved at the end of it when she spotted Lucia smoking against the wall. Like last time, her make-up was smeared round her face and Stacey had to touch up her makeup as well as remove the excess black from around her cheeks.

"There, I don't mean to blow my own trumpet, but I am a miracle maker. No one would even know how wasted you are!" Stacey winked at Lucia but all she could do was stare straight ahead. "Fucking hell, babe, I think you better go and do a line to perk yourself up."

Lucia didn't reply, instead she got up and headed towards the toilets. Before she had a chance to go downstairs, Jorge appeared in front of them, clipboard in hand. The whole room went quiet and everyone instantly stopped what they were doing. Stacey nearly dropped her make-up brush when she noticed Lucia standing directly in front of him.

"Right dancers, we have an opening to do and this year it's going to be the best one there ever was. We have over five thousand people walking through our doors tonight and they're all going to be looking at you. You girls are the face of Amnesia, that means you must deliver. Amnesia is the best club in the world so let's make sure we all keep it that way. Right the groups; I've anointed you all with a letter. The first time we go out, it's all of us A, B, C and D. We dance for ten minutes together. It will be crowded so stay safe, no pushing! Afterwards group A will stay behind and dance for fifteen minutes, then group B then C and then D." Jorge eyes fell upon Lucia with a look which seemed to be a mixture of relief and shock.

"Each group dances for fifteen minutes. Understood? Water and towels are waiting after, as well as drink vouchers. The groups are written on the board so make sure you take note of it. I want all my dancers turning up for their group slot. OK?" Jorge repeated himself in Spanish then German. After his three speeches, he was so riled up that no one dared to move; catching his breath he looked at each girl expectantly. "What are you waiting for *Chicas?* We only have five minutes till we start. *Vamos!*" Jorge shouted as he pointed to the stage.

The changing room was thrown into chaos as the girls started to prepare for the opening show. Suddenly Stacey had girls in front of her with make-up disasters that needed to be addressed. She tried to deal with each one as quickly as possible, and in all the commotion she lost sight of Lucia. She prayed she was somewhere trying to sort herself out. The music was pumping through the room and the countdown was on. Putting the finishing touches to the last girl she stood up and examined the queue of dancers waiting to go on stage. To her relief, Lucia was leaning against a wide-eyed

Petra. Stacey followed the girls and Jorge onto the stage, making sure she wasn't seen in the sidelines.

She stood with baited breath as the dancers ventured out onto the beam. It was three in the morning and thousands of people were dancing underneath them. The music went quiet as the girls and Jorge lined themselves up. The only noise in the club was coming from the cheers of the clubbers down below. Jets of nitrogen oxide gas were dispelled from several cannons making a loud whooshing sound as the white smoke expelled itself onto the dancers. At the same time, the gas was dispersed through the crowd below, causing them to scream. Stacey felt a shiver work through her body. Then the screaming stopped and the room went silent as everyone waited for the DJ's cue.

For all this time I'm watching you

And now I fell in love with you

For all this time,

For all this time...

The music built into a crescendo and the crowd's cheers, screams and whistles started again. Lucia was still hanging onto Petra and somehow, they'd both managed to get away with swaying together. The crowd below was going crazy for the girls and for Jorge, who was displaying his impressive six pack.

Ten minutes soon passed, and Jorge gave the signal for team A to stay. It was obvious that Lucia's grip on Petra was the only thing keeping her going and Stacey could see that Petra was trying to stay behind but Jorge was having none of it and shooed her off stage.

"What was all that about?" Stacey heard him say as he walked Petra off.

"You are not team A and you know it. Why are you trying to cover for Lucia? She is perfectly capable of dancing on her own."

Stacey glanced out onto the beam then, her eyes drawn to Lucia who had completely frozen. She wasn't even trying to dance and Stacey could see the other girls next to her telling her to move but it was pointless, she seemed to be in some sort of trance.

"What is she doing?" Jorge asked as he ran backstage, his face turning bright red.

"Dance, Lucia, fucking dance," Stacey hissed, as Lucia held onto the rail and stepped slowly from side to side.

The clubbers below were shouting 'dance' at her and soon it was being chanted across the crowd, yet Lucia didn't move. Unable to take anymore, Jorge caught her attention and beckoned her off stage. Stacey could feel her cheeks burn up, Lucia and she came as a team and whatever she did, looked bad on both of them. She couldn't believe their jobs could be over before they had even begun. Jorge took Lucia into the corner of the changing room. Stacey tried to approach them, but Jorge put up his hand, stopping her coming any closer. Lucia looked spaced out as Jorge spoke, her eyes fixated on the floor. Jorge was getting more and more heated, he grabbed Lucia's face pulling it to him, so her eyes met his own. Stacey glanced around the changing room for help and saw that a few girls had stopped in their tracks, but no one dared to come close. Lucia pulled away from him, her face full of venom as she said something to him which caused his whole body to go rigid. He shouted at her in what Stacey assumed was Spanish before storming off.

"Lucia. What happened? What did he say?" There was a sadness in Lucia's eyes as she turned to Stacey.

"He told me not to dance here again. Told me to leave immediately." Lucia's voice quivered as she spoke.

"Well you did nearly ruin the opening, babe. He's not going to fire you though. Just sober yourself up and try to get back up there in half an hour OK? Just lay off the coke. You'll be alright."

"He looked at me like I was a piece of shit! I don't need him. I have plenty of clubs that will hire me. I am a star!" Her voice slurred as she said this and Stacey resisted the urge to tell her how ridiculous she sounded.

"Do you want me to come home with you?"

"Home?" Lucia asked, her face screwed up like she had just heard something completely preposterous.

"Well I thought you might want to sleep it off. We can talk to Jorge tomorrow and explain everything. I don't have much work left here to do here, so I'm sure it will be OK."

"No way! I am not going home. This is the opening party and I am going to have fun. Fuck Jorge!"

Stacey's eyes widened at Lucia's outburst; she'd never seen her so defiant.

"I don't think that's a good idea, babe. You're in no fit state."

"Fit state? I'm fine! I want to go party. You stay here. I come to find you, OK?"

"Are you serious, Lucia?"

Lucia examined herself in the mirror, wiping away the smudges from around her eyes she applied some gloss then grabbed the drinks vouchers off the side and headed towards the stairs.

"Lucia! Lucia! Where are you going?"

"I'm sorry, baby, but I'm gonna have some fun. Please don't worry about me." With that she headed out of the door as Stacey stood there in shock.

"Yeah that's right think about yourself!" she shouted after her, as Lucia slammed the door.

"Don't think you're going anywhere." Stacey felt herself jump as she heard Jorge's voice from behind her.

"No, course not. I'm staying here." She could feel the anger emitting from Jorge's body as his eyes bored into the door Lucia had just disappeared into. Happy that she hadn't been fired, Stacey started cleaning her brushes.

"You won't be needing them." His voice was stern and instantly Stacey put down the brushes. "No more make-up tonight."

Stacey stood there unable to decide whether she should argue it out, or just leave. She could feel the tears brimming up inside her but vowed to herself to stay strong.

"OK, no problem. I'll get ready to go."

"No, that's not what I mean. I need you to dance for me tonight, Stacey. With Lucia gone we are now short of girls."

Stacey felt her whole body go rigid at his request. *He wanted her to dance for the club?* She didn't know if she was flattered or scared shitless.

"If you want to keep your job, I need you to do this for me. Do you understand?"

Stacey nodded, not knowing how else to respond. She couldn't get the image of the high beam out of my head. *How was she supposed to dance on that?*

"You're in team D, so you need to be dancing on stage in less than thirty minutes."

"You know I can't dance, right? I told you, remember? Plus, I don't have anything appropriate to wear." She looked down at her white vest top and denim shorts in dismay.

"Stop with this stupid talk. You can do this, you must do this, anyways you don't have a choice, so you better learn fast. If you value your job here you must learn to be adaptable. You now have twenty-eight minutes."

"What about Lucia?" Stacey asked, hoping Jorge would realize how stupid he was being and bring her back.

"Even though she has disgraced me, I will make sure she is looked after so you don't have to worry about her. Let Carmen do your make-up and the other girls might have something you can wear. Don't let me down, OK?" He flicked his hair to the side and strutted away from Stacey, heading out of the same door Lucia had disappeared into.

Stacey gazed at herself despairingly in the mirror, her hair was poking out at the sides and the make-up she had applied earlier had completely disappeared. There was no way she would be able to fit in with all the other beautiful dancers. Out of the corner of her eye she noticed someone staring at her; turning her head she saw Carmen, her stare decidedly softer than previously.

"Come," she said, beckoning her towards her chair.

"I surrender. I don't know how you're going to sort this out but if you do then hats off to you." Stacey plonked herself down on the chair, her hands slightly shaken as the adrenalin coursed through her body.

"Wow," Carmen exclaimed as she looked Stacey up and down. "This is going to take a lot of work."

"Yeah cheers," Stacey said, examining her freckled face in the mirror. It took fifteen minutes of preening and poking, till Carmen let Stacey look at herself. The person staring back in the mirror was unrecognizable from before. Her frizzing hair was now hanging in gleaming curls and her eyes and lips were enhanced to their fullest, making her look almost doll-like.

"So much better now. In fact actually beautiful," Carmen said in surprise. "Now don't waste time staring at yourself, you have to get a costume and fast." Stacey went around the whole changing room, begging and pleading until she managed to obtain a blue sequinned bikini top and a pair of black hot pants that didn't leave much to the imagination.

She even managed to persuade a Spanish girl to lend her spare shoes even though they were a size smaller than what she wore. She couldn't help but stare at herself as she rubbed her glossy pink lips and pouted in front of the mirror. She felt amazing, the only downside to it all was that she was going to have to dance in front of thousands of people.

Her legs felt like jelly and she just knew she was going to make an idiot of herself.

"Team D get ready, you have one minute!" Jorge's eyes fell upon Stacey. "Stacey, is that you? Wow Carmen! Good job, that was not easy."

"Thanks," Stacey replied, the sarcasm evident in her voice.

"Now show me what you are made of *Ingles. Vamos*! Team D!"

Stacey followed the other girls onto the beam, swapping with the previous dancers.

Instantly she felt herself get dizzy; trying to block out her nerves she concentrated on the music. The DJ was playing the new version of the old school classic, *Pump up the Jam*.

Stacey had heard her mum play it countless times growing up and luckily she knew the beats well. That didn't stop her from freezing up momentarily as she looked at the faces below and then at the other girls who had already started to dance. All of them looked so graceful, she suddenly felt completely out of place. She tried to focus back in on the song.

At first all she could manage was a shuffle from side to side, then her steps became longer and more fluid. Feeling brave, she grabbed the bar in front of her and shimmied up and down it, wiggling her hips. She soon found herself moving to the music naturally like she would at a club but better. If she'd held up her hand it would be clearly shaking but the adrenalin had taken over and she carried on regardless of her nerves. She was surprised to find herself dancing in time with the beats. She saw people looking up at her and it threw her off her balance a little. What if they realised she wasn't a real dancer and booed her off? Then she saw a man in the crowd below smile at her, then another blow her kiss. She couldn't help herself from smiling, which brought her even more attention. Her smile became even wider till eventually she was beaming from ear to ear. She'd never felt so confident standing in front of a huge crowd of people. If only the bullies could see her now, they'd always teased her because of her ginger hair, freckles and hand-me-down clothes but now she was dancing in front of thousands of people in one of the most coolest clubs in the world. Stacey twirled around to face the VIP area behind her. She nearly stopped in her tracks when she spotted Lucia, talking intensely with a dodgy looking man with a slicked back ponytail. Stacey saw him put a hand on Lucia's knee and lean closer into her. She wondered for a moment if it was Nico, yet on closer inspection he wasn't as handsome as Lucia had described, in fact with his shifty eyes and greased hair, there was something a little bit creepy about him. Lucia was drinking from a champagne glass, her hands constantly touching her nostrils as she spoke. She looked completely out of it as she draped her arms around the shady-looking guy. Stacey wanted to drag her off him but she was stuck were she was. She forced herself to get lost in the beats of the music again and as the crowd cheered in her direction she couldn't help but look on the bright side. She was in one of the best clubs in the world, dancing in front of thousands of adoring people.

If Lucia wasn't so out of it she wouldn't be here, so in a way she was grateful. So what if they were being hunted down by some psycho drug dealer whose stuff Lucia and she had been getting high on? This was Ibiza and she was sure worse things had happened on an island built around hedonistic pursuits, hadn't it?

6

Stacey was out of breath and her body was drowning in sweat, yet she felt completely exhilarated as she stepped off the ledge she had been dancing on for the last twenty minutes. The other dancers were wrapping tissue paper around their heads in the changing room to mop up the excess perspiration and grabbing a roll, Stacey followed suit. Once her heartbeat had slowed and her skin had cooled down, her thoughts turned to Lucia and the mysterious man she had been so deep in conversation with. Stacey couldn't just leave her with him, anything could happen to her in that state and she could never forgive herself if it did.

The club was heaving with people as Stacey negotiated her way upstairs desperate to find Lucia. She did a double take when she saw *him*, the guy who had rescued her from Space. He was leant against the wall, his face furrowed towards the mobile phone in his hand. Not wanting to lose him again, she quickly headed over to him, nearly tripping over a raised platform in the process.

"Hello, stranger," was all Stacey could muster, as she stood breathless in front of him.

He glanced up from his phone, his brown eyes were guarded as he stared at her.

"Do I know you?"

Stacey instantly felt awkward; *of course he didn't remember her.*

"Fucking hell, it's you, the girl who collapsed on the ground! Wow! You look a lot better than the last time I saw you."

"Yep that's me," Stacey answered, feeling her face flush as the memory of her drooling uncontrollably came flooding into her thoughts.

"I was only thinking about you the other day. I felt guilty for not staying around and checking you were OK."

"Well it wasn't pretty, but I managed to sober up, eventually. Thank you by the way, I don't know what would have happened if you hadn't come along and rescued me."

"Just call me your knight in shining armour." He smiled at Stacey, revealing two dimples either side of his chiselled face. He was even sexier than she remembered and Stacey couldn't help but stare at him. His eyes burned into hers as he noticed her watching him, and Stacey quickly averted her gaze to the ground.

"Well, knight in shining armour, thanks again, I owe you. I would offer you a drink but I've got to find my friend."

"Don't be soft! I've got a table full of drinks. If you promise to remain on two feet this time I'll take you with me. You might even be able to spot your mate from there." His brown eyes sparkled at Stacey as he looked her up and down.

"I could do with a drink and my friend isn't exactly in the most cooperative mood," she replied, his obvious flirting helping to dispel her anxiety. "But first I need to know your name. I don't know whether you told it to me or not but I haven't got a clue what it is. Sorry."

"Oh, you want my name?" He paused and looked around the room as if considering his options. "It's Aaron."

"Well it's nice to meet you, Aaron." She held out her hand and he brought it towards his lips and kissed it.

"Nice to meet you again, Stacey."

"You remembered my name?"

"How could I forget?" he said, making the heat rise to Stacey's face.

"You here alone?" she asked, feeling stupidly clichéd for doing so.

"Just a few friends, you?"

"Well I'm working here, so."

"You're a dancer?"

"Well, a make-up artist really but I'm filling in for my friend who decided to get so wasted she couldn't even dance! Suppose it serves me right for doing the same to her at Space."

"Ibiza gets everyone like it in the end. Better lay off them happy pills yourself, you don't wanna be falling off that beam!"

"Well, well, well I leave you for ten minutes and you're already gassing with some bird!"

Stacey turned to see a girl with platinum blonde hair and a neon pink dress head towards them. She tried to hide her disappointment as the woman with the ballsy Liverpudlian accent approached them.

"It's fucking roasting in here tonight! I've got sweat in places I never knew I could sweat in!"

"Classy," Aaron said, his eyes flicking over to Stacey uneasily.

Stacey examined the pair stood in front of her; she had to admit they did make an odd match.

"So you gonna introduce us or not?" She looked at Aaron expectantly causing him to shuffle from side to side.

"Stacey, meet my cousin, Kylie."

Stacey breathed a sigh of relief and held out her hand, as Kylie leant into her.

"Come here," she said, pulling Stacey towards her and kissing her on both cheeks.

"Nice to meet you, love. You kept this one quiet. She's gorgeous!"

"We met in Space."

"Oh! Are you the one he rescued from the floor?"

Stacey instantly felt her cheeks flush as Aaron smirked in her direction.

"Yep, that would be me."

"Aw, no wonder, she's a cutie." She turned to Stacey giving her one of her megawatt, white smiles. "Makes a change for him to meet a girl, normally he's just moping around being miserable and giving me a hard time." She rolled her eyes and put her arm around Stacey. "Right come on, we've got a table in the VIP with far too many drinks. I know me cousin would like it if youse joined us!"

Stacey glanced at Aaron who raised his eyebrows and let out a *do what she says* smile, in her direction.

"Well I do have to be on stage in thirty minutes."

"That's loadsa time! Come on I'm not taking no for an answer."

"I really should make sure my friend's OK. She's in a right pickle."

"Everyone's in a right pickle, this is Ibiza!"

Aaron gave her a pleading glance that Stacey found hard to refuse. She reasoned with herself that it was just one drink with a man who'd rescued her and who she hadn't been able to get out of her thoughts since. Surely, it was her turn now to let her hair down and have some fun.

"OK one drink but that's it."

With his hand entwined in Stacey's, Aaron led her to a staircase to the right of the bar.

The room was so hidden away you wouldn't even know it existed, yet there were two huge security guards guarding the entrance. As soon as they saw Aaron and Kylie they were all smiles and didn't hesitate to pull back the red rope that had been cornering off the private entrance. The space reminded Stacey of one of the boxes at the theatre and even though it was completely tucked away, you could still see everything from the dancers to the DJ box. There were four girls inside, all wearing brightly coloured short dresses mimicking a human rainbow as they leant against the rail overlooking the dance floor below. They all turned around as Stacey entered, their eyes scanning her unashamedly from top to bottom.

"Here you are, welcome to my humble abode, *mi casa, su casa* and all that. Don't mind the girls, they're harmless. Now what will you be having, champagne or vodka, princess?" Aaron pointed to the table in the middle of the room with two buckets on it, one

138

containing a clear glass bottle of vodka and the other a pink-labelled champagne.

"I'll have a glass of champagne," she said, remembering how she'd liked the taste of it at one of theatre's after-show *soirees.*

"Wohoo! Let's get this party started! Don't worry girls, this is a friend of our Aaron's.

"She's already made him smile once tonight, so she can't be half bad! And well done cuz, you melt, you nearly lost this one. You can thank me later!"

Aaron was now laughing and so was Kylie and her girlfriends. It was infectious and before she knew it Stacey was laughing along with them.

"Cheers everyone!" Kylie shouted, bringing the other girls into chorus.

"Cheers!" Stacey raised her glass towards Aaron who held up his bottle of water towards her.

"Tell me that is not water in your hand, is it? With all these drinks here?"

"Yep, your eyes are not deceiving you! I am on the water. Someone has got to stay in control. My cousin is the biggest handful when she's drunk, even worse than you!"

"Well you can't be rescuing everyone all the time and she seems like a big enough girl to me. Come on, one won't do you any harm."

Aaron stared into her eyes hesitantly then putting down his water he shrugged his shoulders.

"How I ever thought I could get away with being a good boy when you're around I don't know!" He exclaimed, winking at her then walking over to the table.

Stacey watched as his impressive shoulders reached over to the vodka bottle. His face was entirely concentrated on what he was doing and his cheekbones and jaw protruded even more magnificently than before, yet there was a sadness in the way he moved his body. His eyes caught Stacey's own, they were dark and guarded but he quickly changed them to a more softer stare as he smiled at her.

"Cheers." He raised his glass towards hers and headed over to the railings as the girls huddled on the sofa. Stacey looked out onto the dance floor as Aaron stood next to her, neither of them saying a thing.

"How comes you're in Ibiza then Aaron?" Stacey asked, noticing his body go rigid.

"Oh you know, partying and stuff," he said, with a more casual air than he appeared to possess.

"Drinking water?" she asked, not entirely sold by his response.

"I told you, tonight I'm looking after my cousin. God you're a nosy one, you!"

Stacey could see he was feeling uncomfortable with her questions and it made her want to know even more.

"So what do you do back home then to afford all this? You must be minted!"

"More questions? If you must know I work for my parents' business."

"Doing what?"

"Doing none of your business girl! Now stop with the questions, OK?"

"Why all the mystery?" Stacey asked, not wanting to let it drop.

"What mystery?" Aaron asked, his smile not reaching his eyes.

"You. I spot you here, with all this and it's like you don't want to tell me anything about yourself."

"Maybe you should keep your nose out of stuff that doesn't concern you then."

The whole club was thrown into darkness and the music came to a stop. Screams and howls from the clubbers below broke the silence as the lights came back on, spotlighting the DJ box.

"It's fucking Sven Vath! Go on lad! Annihilate it!" Kylie shouted from behind them.

"Look I've got to go. It will be my turn to dance soon and I still need to find Lucia."

Stacey put her drink down and walked towards the rope. She felt Aaron grab her, his touch sending shivers throughout her body.

"Don't go."

"Look, Aaron, I've got enough crap of my own to deal with right now." She turned away from him as she felt herself welling up.

"I didn't mean to be off with you. You're the prettiest, craziest girl I've met in a long time and I want to get to know you. It's just my life is complicated right now." Aaron spoke into her ear, his breath on her skin made her whole body tremble. He pulled her to him so his face met her own. His eyes were so dark and inviting, for a split second Stacey didn't care that he had been acting so guardedly. He took her face into his hands and leant in towards her. His lips touched hers and she felt the brush of his light stubble against her mouth. It was the most passionate kiss she'd ever had, but conscious that Kylie and the others would be watching, she pulled away. He smiled at her and stroked her face, she felt shy in front of him and pulled her gaze away from his. Then she laughed and he laughed back, his hand sought hers and they looked across the balcony at the crazy crowd below.

"Is that your friend?" Aaron asked, his horrified expression matching Stacey's.

Lucia was draped over the same creepy guy but this time Stacey noticed a group of men surrounding them, whose serious expressions didn't seem to be giving off the party vibe.

"Oh my God! I can't believe she is still there with him and who are those guys? I've got to go help her. She is completely out of it. She's already been fired tonight, not that it has slowed her down. It just seems to have made her worse."

"Do you know that man?" She could hear the concern in Aaron's voice as he spoke to her.

"No way! He must just be some random. I better go and check on her. Plus, I've got to get back to work. I'm sure I was supposed to be dancing with that group."

Aaron was still fixated on Lucia and the guy with the slicked back hair, who was now pouring her another drink.

"You need to get her away from that guy."

"I know, he looks like a right sleaze."

"No. I'm being deadly serious. That guy is, well just believe me, you do not want your friend with him, at all." Aaron's body had gone stiff as he stepped back from the balcony and beckoned her to follow him. "Are you positive you don't know him?" His dark eyes had a burning intensity to them and Stacey felt like she was being interrogated.

"No, of course not. Why would you think that?"

"Don't lie to me, Stacey. Has he asked you to come here?"

"No. I swear. What's all this about?"

"Tell me the truth, Stacey."

"I am telling you the truth. What is up with you? Look, thanks for the drink, it's been a pleasure but I've got to be off," she fired back with all the sarcasm she could muster. *Who did this guy think he was? Mr. I can't tell you who I am.*

Stacey walked towards the rope and Aaron didn't attempt to stop her. A tear crept out of her eye as she walked past the security guards. *Why was everything in her life so complicated?* She walked down the stairs, heading towards Lucia who she had decided to drag home if she wouldn't come willingly.

"Stacey! Where the fuck have you been? I've been looking for you everywhere. You need to dance. You missed your last slot and someone kindly danced twice for you. Don't let it happen again."

"I can't Jorge. I've got to get Lucia, she's in trouble."

"You need to dance. That is all you need to worry about. Now where is that *idiota*?"

"She's over there, on one of the tables."

"And she is in trouble because?"

"She is wasted and the guy she's with is bad news."

Jorge laughed to himself.

"Yes, this seems like Lucia."

"Well let's just leave her and hope she isn't raped or anything then," Stacey retorted, not hiding the irritation in her voice.

"OK, OK. I'll send security to look out for her. Now can you please just dance?

"Otherwise there will be no second chances. You and Lucia will be out, end of."

"It's not like I have a choice then," she answered, letting out a deep sigh.

"That's a good girl. Now go! You have five minutes before you're on stage." He pushed her towards the changing room.

Back stage was like a mini party was taking place, everyone seemed in good spirits and Stacey suddenly felt very envious of them. After all, none of them had a big stash of drugs to get back to an angry dealer, or a best friend who was getting high like it was going out of fashion, or had just finally met the man of their dreams, only to find out he was completely deranged. Her life was one big mess! All the dancers were lining up and Stacey joined them. She stepped carefully across the beam to cheers and shouts but her eyes were focused on the table where she'd seen Lucia. Neither she, the weird guy or his entourage was there. Everyone had started dancing and not wanting to get into any more trouble she joined in, twirling herself against the horizontal pole that ran across the outside of the beam. She couldn't resist glancing up to the boxed section she'd been in before; the girls were still there but there was no sign of Aaron. Both of the people that mattered to her had vanished into thin air, yet she was stuck dancing in front of thousands of people. With no other choice, Stacey let the music take over her body and danced until once again, she was allowed back into the messed-up reality that was her life.

7

"Stacey! Come here!"

Stacey had barely had enough time to catch her breath as Jorge called her over to him.

She grabbed a toilet roll and headed over to the back of the changing room where Jorge was standing.

"She has to be taken home. She has let us, and the whole of Amnesia down tonight. I don't even know if we will be having her back." He pointed at Lucia who was slumped on one of the chairs, her hair covering her face.

"Yes of course. I'll get us a taxi."

"Good, get her to call me tomorrow but for now, get her out of my sight."

Stacey nodded in agreement, her anger towards Lucia rising as she realised all her hard work had been tainted by her selfish behaviour. She walked over to Lucia who lifted her head up and smiled meekly in her direction. Her face was almost devoid of make-up and her hair was matted at the back. Stacey suddenly got a flashback of her mother in the same pose. The similarity between the two made her want to run away as far as possible but her conscience wouldn't let her. Lucia had given her so much in life, she couldn't just turn her back on her.

"You looked fantastic up there, baby." Lucia's voice was hoarse but somehow it sounded beautiful combined with her Italian accent.

"Jorge wants us both to leave."

"Jorge is fine, don't worry."

"Well actually he isn't and we have to go now, so thanks a lot."

"OK we go, I'm sorry, I speak to him tomorrow, OK?"

Apart from explaining to the taxi driver where they needed to go, both Lucia and Stacey remained silent on the way home. Stacey still couldn't get the image of Lucia hunched over out of her head. *Had she just escaped one bad situation for another?* It was starting to get light as they entered the reception of their building. Stacey was relieved to see that the weird manageress wasn't around as she followed a stumbling Lucia up the stairs. Stacey locked the door behind her and watched as Lucia placed her bag down and lit a cigarette.

"So you going to tell me about that guy you've been talking to all night?"

"You mean Nico's boss, Salvatore?"

"The one you were flirting with in the VIP."

"I wasn't flirting with him, he is a friend who helped me understand a lot of things tonight." Lucia voice was still hoarse but it had more strength in it than before.

"What did he make you understand?"

"About Nico and I and why he acted so strange to me."

"You saw Nico?"

"Yes, but fuck him, seriously." It suddenly dawned on Stacey that it wasn't just the drugs that had made Lucia go AWOL, it was obvious she was upset by something to do with Nico.

"What happened? What did he say?"

Lucia's eyes started to well up as she took a long drag on her cigarette.

"OK, OK, I tell you but it's the last time I talk about him, OK?"

"OK, no problem. What happened?"

"I saw Salvatore in the VIP. I knew that Nico would be around so I go there. He wasn't there though, just Salvatore who told me to not waste my time with him because, wait for it, Nico is married and has been all the time for three years! Three years!"

"No way! Did you see him after that?"

"Yes the bastard comes to the table but I run away. He chases me and I confront him.

"He finally admits to me the truth, but says to me that he is not in love with his wife anymore. Can you believe? All this time he tried to play me. I tell him I don't want anything to do with him and you know what he says to this? That he loves me and wants to leave his wife but she is sick with depression. What am I suppose to do with that? I tell him that I never want to see him again, that he is a fucking liar and that I will personally tell his wife what he do with me if he ever tries to talk to me again. Thanks to God he leaves me as I was this close to hitting him."

"Bloody hell, that sounds awful. You poor thing."

"It's OK. Really, I actually feel relief this time. I was thinking he didn't want me but now I know he is just an arsehole like the rest. Anyways more important is that I speak to Salvatore after. He can definitely, one hundred percent, help us with the drugs."

"You told him about the drugs?"

"No, but I know he has connections in the mafia which means he can protect us. I always thought he was too much but we speak a lot tonight and he is OK, really. I've got his number but I wanted to wait to ask you first."

"I'm sorry but I don't think it's a good idea. You can't possibly think you can trust him after one conversation."

"And you have a better plan?"

"No, but I'm sure this Salvatore isn't a good guy. I was with that guy who rescued me from Space earlier, he told me to stay away from him. In fact, he freaked out when he saw you together."

"You saw *him* again? How the fuck does he know about Salvatore?"

"I don't know, but he told me that you shouldn't be anywhere near him and that he was bad news."

"So you wanna that I trust this man I don't know? 'Cause you like him? What if *he* is the bad guy, eh?"

Stacey thought back to the argument between Aaron and herself. He had completely freaked over Salvatore, but apart from that he did *seem* like a good guy. Then again, what did she actually know about him? Lucia reached inside her bag and placed a plastic baggie containing white powder on the table.

"Where did you get that from?"

"Stop to worry, it wasn't from your precious drugs."

"Where did you get it then?"

"Salvatore gave it to me." Stacey let out a big sigh.

"You're not going to sniff it now, are you?"

"I need your permission?" Using her Amnesia promotions card, Lucia started to make herself a line.

"Lucia, seriously, let's just go to bed."

"What's the point to sleep when we have this problem?" She inhaled the line into her nostril and then leant back. "I'm going to call him. He promised he would be there for me if."

"Don't do it," Stacey said, as Lucia pulled out her phone. Lucia ignored her and started to dial. Not knowing what came over her, Stacey strode towards Lucia and whacked the phone out of her hand, sending it flying across the table.

"You stupid bitch! Why the fuck did you do that?"

"'Cause if you hadn't of noticed, there are two of us in this situation, not just you. I've got a bad feeling about this guy. Aaron said…"

"Who the hell is *he* to say about Salvatore? You've gone crazy, throwing my things about.

No, I'm definitely calling him, he will be able to sort this mess out and if you don't like it, then go back to where you came from, OK?"

"Oh do what you like, Lucia, I've had it. Just call him and get rid, this shit is tearing us apart."

Lucia retrieved her phone and headed towards the bathroom.

"No, no, no, no, no! *Cazzo voi?*"

"What's happened?" Stacey asked, as she ran towards Lucia.

"It's fucking gone! Someone has been here and taken it! I can't believe! *Did you tell him?*" Lucia asked, as she frantically searched the dusty foam underneath the bath.

"No, of course I didn't. I didn't tell anyone. Did you?"

"I don't tell anybody."

"Whoever has taken it, did it whilst we were at Amnesia." Stacey picked up the panel and placed it back into the slot. Apart from the foam on the floor there was no trace that they'd had any sort of break in. "What I really wanna know, is how the fuck did they get through the door without leaving a mark?"

"I don't know. I don't know," Lucia said, as she got up and peered through a crack in the blinds.

"Don't, Luce! They could still be outside."

"What the fuck we gonna do?"

"The way I see it there isn't a lot we can do, but hold tight and see what happens, maybe it's gone back to the rightful owner. Either way I think we're soon going to find out."

Lucia walked back over to the table and cut herself another line.

"What *are* you doing?"

She leant over and inhaled the powder and choked as it hit the back of her throat.

"For fuck's sake!"

There was a knock at the door. Stacey could feel herself trembling as she looked around the room for a weapon. Lucia stood frozen in shock, the rolled up note still in her hand.

"Lucia stash it, quick!" Thinking it could danger at the door, Stacey put the kettle on and reached for her deodorant. She tiptoed towards the door and looked through the spy hole, it was Summer. Surprised and relieved, Stacey put down the aerosol and opened the door.

Without a single greeting, Summer stepped straight into the room, her face turned up like she had smelt something bad.

"Don't mind u," Stacey said, her eyes falling upon Lucia who had covered up the coke and was now pretending to make tea.

"Where are they?" Summer asked as she walked around the room, her eyes scanning every crevice.

"What are you talking about?" Stacey asked, apprehensive to what her answer was going to be.

"It's messy in here, which won't do, especially as we have two more guests coming here today."

"What? I thought we had booked this room for a week? You can't just kick us out!"

"I think you'll find I can do whatever I like. Especially as there were two men spotted letting themselves into your apartment last night. Now, I don't know what you think this is, but we don't have unauthorized guests here. I told your friend this and so as you failed to keep to it, you are being asked to evacuate the premises. You have till this afternoon."

"There were men in our apartment last night?"

"Don't try to act innocent, they were seen coming out of your room."

"Well that's funny 'cause we were working last night, as you know, and now our room has been broken into, so before you go accusing us, maybe we should call the police and find these men." Stacey realised that she had gone a little too far with her protest. After all, how could they call the police for the missing cocaine that never belonged to them in the first place?

"Robbed? That's impossible! Now I know you're lying! Nobody can get through our doors. This place is one hundred percent impenetrable."

"Well we didn't give anyone permission to be in our room, so you're going to have to believe us."

"So what is it these men have stolen from you then?"

"Our money." Lucia spoke up from the back of the room.

"So they stole your money? How much did they exactly steal?"

"Five hundr…"

"…Three hundred." Stacey and Lucia said, almost simultaneously.

"Sounds like you girls should have gotten your stories straight before you tried to lie to me," Summer retorted, with what Stacey was sure was a glint in her eyes. "You're lucky I don't kick you both out now, without your stuff. Now hurry up and pack, I've just moved forward your deadline. You now have an hour to get out. Otherwise, I will have you escorted off the premises without your belongings or your deposit. I'll be waiting downstairs so no funny business. Oh and hand over your keys, you won't be needing them."

Both Stacey and Lucia stood there staring at Summer in shock as she grabbed their keys off the side. Lucia's eyes were wide and her face was devoid of any emotion. Stacey wished she wasn't so wasted, normally she was the one to get them out of any altercations but it was like the old Lucia had faded away and there was only a shell left.

"Right, ladies, I will be seeing you both in less than an hour from now. Oh and don't leave any mess otherwise I will be deducting it from your deposit." With that she smiled and then slammed the door behind her.

Lucia went over to the hidden pile of cocaine on the table, sniffling, she started to make another line.

"What *are* you doing, Lucia? We need to get out of here."

"Yes, I know this, but first I need a line, OK?"

"Don't you think you've had enough? We need to get packing and cleaning."

"Why don't you keep your nose out of my business? If it wasn't for me, you would still be looking after your mamma."

"So you think it's better that I stand back and watch whilst you destroy yourself, and not even challenge it?"

"Destroy myself? You are being too dramatic! You think you know everything, but you don't. You need to grow up and realize not everyone gonna be like your mamma!"

Stacey watched in dismay as Lucia bent over the table and sniffed another line. She couldn't take it anymore; reaching over she grabbed the baggy of coke and emptied the whole lot into the sink.

"What the fuck have you done?" Lucia said, pushing her out of the way.

"What I should have done ages ago. You're not thinking straight anymore!"

"You fucking bitch," Lucia screamed, the whites of her eyes dominating her face as she lunged towards Stacey, causing her to crash against the sink. Stacey pushed her back in defence and Lucia crumpled to the ground, hitting her head against the cupboard on her way down.

"I'm sorry, but I had to do that, you wouldn't listen, Luce." Stacey reached down and offered her a hand.

"Get away from me! You're fucking crazy."

Stacey started to gather her belongings from around the room and place them into her suitcase. She didn't have a clue where or what she was going to do, but she knew she needed to get away from Lucia and the apartment, as quickly as possible.

"You going to leave?" Lucia pulled herself up and gripped onto the kitchen side.

"Where do you think you are going anyways? You have no money, no clue, no idea, no nothing."

At least I won't have to put up with another junkie, Stacey thought, as she counted the measly amount of change in her purse.

"Until you can admit you have a problem, Lucia, then I can't be part of your life. I've done it for too long now with my mum. I'm sorry but you're on your own."

Tears were falling down Stacey's face as she packed the last of her stuff into her case.

Lucia had started packing, too, but with a lot less vigour; her face looked so miserable and beaten down it almost made Stacey want to stop packing. She couldn't feel sorry for her though, not after the way she had just attacked her. She didn't need any more abuse in her life and until Lucia cleaned her act up she was definitely better off alone. Grabbing the last of her stuff she headed towards the door.

"Where are you going to go, Stacey? Come on, don't be stupid. Come with me, Salvatore will let us stay in his villa. We can be safe there till we sort something."

The last thing Stacey wanted was for Lucia to stay at Salvatore's but there was no point trying to warn her, it would just be falling on deaf ears.

"I'm sorry but I can't do this, Luce. Call me when you sort yourself out."

"You know what? Go! See how far you get without me."

It was all the justification Stacey needed; gathering her bags she walked out the door.

Summer was on the phone as Stacey walked past but she kept walking, she didn't want to stop for anyone. She walked out onto the street with her suitcase and bag. It took all her strength not to burst into tears. Taking a deep breath, she stood a little taller and examined her surroundings. There was a couple in the distance, standing on the corner of the street with their thumbs pointing towards the moving traffic. Stacey watched as a car pulled over and they jumped in. She remembered what Lucia had said about hitchhiking being the norm in Ibiza and a plan started to formulate in her head. Not knowing whether she was being crazy or resourceful, she held her thumb in the air. She might be alone, broke and homeless but she wasn't about to give up.

Separate Ways

1

Stacey tried her hardest to muster up some enthusiasm as she looked up at the hill that marked the beginning of the West End. Somewhere amongst the bars, clubs, take-away restaurants and shops, she would have to find a place she could call home. It wasn't going to be easy, considering she only had sixty euros to her name. Using the last of her strength, she wheeled her suitcase to the nearest café. It looked relatively cheap and had a great view overlooking the promenade, so even though her funds were low, she decided to sit down. She hadn't slept yet, and she needed something substantial inside of her if she was going to scour the whole of San Antonio. She was relieved to see a ham and cheese *bocadillo* was only two euros-fifty, and a cappuccino one euro-fifty. As she waited for her order, her thought turned to her fight with Lucia. She couldn't believe someone who was supposed to be her friend had turned on her like that. It was obvious she would go straight to Salvatore, and even though Aaron had warned her against him, Stacey was still glad she had somewhere to go to, the state she was in. She thought about trying to ring her but she just couldn't bring herself to do it.

"Hi, is this seat taken?" Stacey looked up from her coffee.

Stood in front of her was probably one of the fattest men she'd seen since arriving in Ibiza.

The way she was feeling she really didn't want to converse with anyone but he was wearing an Eden t-shirt and had a handful of flyers, which meant he knew a lot more about San Antonio than she did.

"No, it's just me."

"Cheers, love. I'm bloody parched! Are you alright?"

Stacey instantly covered her cheek with her hand.

"Oh yeah, I'm fine. Just watching the world go by."

"Oh, lucky you, I'm Matt by the way. I work for Eden doing all things promotional. You on holiday here, sweetie?"

"I wish," Stacey said, pointing to her bulging suitcase.

"Don't we all love, don't we all."

Stacey smiled at Matt, he seemed harmless enough and it was nice to talk to somebody who wasn't off their head.

"I'm Stacey."

"Nice to meet you, love. Where you staying then?"

"I haven't got a clue," she said, not having the luxury of being guarded.

"You didn't book a hotel?"

"No, to be totally honest with you, I don't have anywhere to stay and no job and hardly any money but I am a hard worker. If you know of anything going?" In theory, she did still have a job at Amnesia but she'd done the maths, there was no way she could take a taxi there every night, pay for accommodation, and food on sixty euros a night. That's if Jorge would even have her back.

"Whoa there, pretty lady. Who do you think I am, a social worker? Everyone on the island is looking for somewhere to stay and work but it's not cheap, love and most of us have to do something extra on the side to stay afloat."

"What do you mean?"

"If you know, you know. You're obviously still a bit green. What I meant is Ibiza is an expensive place to live and all the best jobs and apartments go early on, you've missed the boat by two weeks."

Stacey put her head in her hands and resisted the urge to cry.

"Oh come on, don't get upset. A pretty girl like you, it's easy to make money if you know how."

Stacey looked up at Matt, his face had formed into a smirk.

"OK, whatever dirty thought you've got going on right now, just cut it out. I'm not in the mood to be perved on."

"Oh don't be so silly. You're talking to a friend of Dorothy baby. I'm only interested in perving if it involves a big juicy sausage. Thought that was obvious."

Stacey realised then that she had been so caught up in her own stuff, she'd failed to notice that Matt was obviously gay.

"Wow. Sorry. OK."

"What are you saying? Fat guys can't be gay? We don't all have six packs you know."

"No, no I wasn't saying that at all. My mind's just elsewhere right now. Sorry."

"It's fine, I'm messing with you!"

"Oh, OK, phew! I thought I'd seriously upset you then."

"I shouldn't have wound you up. I can see you're having a bad day."

"Seriously one of the worst. I really need a break, I've got no money and no job."

"Have you ever thought about wiggling about on a pole in your thong whilst men pay you shit loads of money?"

"Stripping? No! Definitely not for me. I couldn't think of anything more petrifying!"

Matt started to laugh.

"Darling, when you see the money, it's easy to become whatever you need to be. One of the girls was telling me she earnt over six hundred euros the other night."

"Really? That is a lot of money for one night."

"Do you at least have somewhere to stay tonight?"

"No, not really."

"Fucking hell, you really are up shit creek without a paddle."

"Yeah, cheers for that."

"Don't worry though, today just might be your lucky day; I've got a mate who works at a hotel. You got any money at all?"

"A little."

"Well I can get you a room for thirty euros but he will do you a deal if you pay for more than one night."

"Well I only have enough for one night."

"Then you can't afford to be fussy! Look I'm not trying to make you feel bad. It wasn't long ago I was out here with no job and nowhere to live. You'll be OK but really you should at least consider checking that club out."

"Really, I'm so grateful for your help. I'm not sure about the stripping but I definitely need somewhere to sleep tonight so if you're still up for taking me to your friend's place I would really appreciate that."

"Sure thing. And don't worry you've got a friend in me now, girlfriend."

Matt grabbed Stacey's suitcase and she followed him up the hill, thankful that things were finally looking up.

2

The sky was starting to turn dark and Stacey's panic over her situation was setting in as she headed back to her hotel room. Earlier on, she'd walked all the way to Café Del Mar, in the hope she could find a job. She'd imagined herself watching the sunset every night whilst listening to chill out music but her dreams had been dashed when all five of the bars along the sunset strip had informed her that their vacancies had been filled. One of the bartenders had advised her to try the West End but she was out of the luck there too. The only jobs left paid pittance, meaning she would barely be able to feed herself, let alone pay for her accommodation. It briefly crossed her mind to ring Lucia but she couldn't bring herself to do it, she was still too angry. That's when she spotted the sign for Temptation, the strip club Matt had mentioned previously. The doors were locked but the neon sign was switched on and as she stood outside, she tried to imagine herself dancing naked in front of random men. The thought absolutely terrified her but with no other opportunities on the horizon, she couldn't see any other choice. The smell of garlic was starting to waft through the streets as happy holidaymakers sat down for dinner.

Overcome with tiredness, hunger and dehydration, Stacey headed back towards the café where she had first arrived. The waiter seemed surprised to see her again, especially when she ordered another cheese and ham sandwich. She was so hungry it barely touched the sides. After she'd finished, she sat at the table and watched the tourists go by, their lives seemed so easy and care free. She took a deep breath and willed herself into action. There were still a few bars she hadn't checked out and on top of that, there were still the two clubs near the roundabout: Eden and Es Paradis to try. Maybe Matt would able to put a word in for her at Eden. With a new sense of hope and a full belly, she made her way across the promenade. Both of the clubs were shut which was unsurprising as it was only nine-thirty.

According to one passerby, they didn't open till past eleven. *Could she wait until eleven to see if they had vacancies? And if she did,* w*ould she even be paid that night?* She walked back to the West End and checked out the three bars she hadn't been to but just like the other bars, they expected her to work for peanuts. Stacey found herself completely torn, it was now half-ten. The last bar she'd tried was directly opposite Temptations and as she walked past it she couldn't resist a peek inside the opened doors.

The first thing she noticed was how dark it was, it reminded her of a dungeon. She found herself wandering inside and noticed there were already a few young boys getting chatted up by scantily-clad women in huge high heels.

"Can I help you?" a Spanish man in his late twenties, with headphones hanging from his neck, asked her.

"Erm. I don't know," she replied, not knowing why she was even in there.

"You're a dancer here?"

She thought about Amnesia, she *had* been a dancer.

"No."

"You come for an audition?"

"I think so," she said, as one of the young boys pulled forty euros from his wallet and handed it to a blonde dancer.

"Well you are or you not. Make up your mind."

Stacey thought about the money she'd just seen and the story of Matt's friend who had made six hundred in one night. If she could make half of what that girl did, after a couple of night's work she could find herself a better job, preferably something to do with make-up.

"Hello?" The Spanish guy brought her out of her trance.

"Yes, sorry. I want to audition if that's OK?"

"OK, you need to speak to the Richard. I get him for you."

"Thanks," she said, the adrenalin that was rushing through her body making her feel shaky. She leant against the wall to steady herself, and watched as the raven-haired girl on stage with tattoos up her arms took her bra off, releasing her huge breasts. She got a few cheers but she didn't smile, instead she arched her back against the pole, accentuating the silhouette of her body.

"Er, hello? Earth calling new-girl."

Stacey realised she'd gone into another trance. The man stood in front of her was wearing a white shirt and tan cargo pants and was nothing at all what she imagined the boss of a strip club to look like.

"OK, glad I've finally got your attention. I'm Richard, the owner of this place. Normally it's Tiggy who does auditions but she went to Cocoon last night and apparently needs to recover. Not that I let all my girls book days off but she has been working solidly for two weeks now."

Stacey instantly noticed Richard's deep and husky northern accent as his sparkly blue eyes met her own.

"Nice to meet you, I'm Stacey."

"Is Stacey your stage name or your real name, sweetheart?"

"Erm, my real name." She felt Richard look her up and down and for a minute. It was not dissimilar to Jorge's inspection yet this time she felt more like he was undressing her with his eyes.

"OK, well I don't need to see you audition. You're pretty and definitely slim, so you've got the job. There are conditions though."

Here we go, she thought to herself.

"There are no sex or sex acts here. We are an English strip club, not an undercover brothel like most of the clubs out here. Also you work at least four nights, you come in on time and leave at either five or six in the morning depending on your shift. Is that OK?"

Richard glared at her, his face poker straight.

"That sounds fair," she replied, relieved that there was nothing more going on in the establishment than taking her clothes off.

"In turn we look after you girls. No trouble will come to you here. We have a free bar, although don't get too fucked, that goes for drugs too. Any problems see me or Tiggy. Is that cool?"

More and more, she was liking this man stood before her, he seemed straight down the line and that's just what she needed on an island full of crazy people.

"Yes that's fine. Can I start tonight?"

"Eager one! No problem, Honey. I take it you have an outfit?"

She'd completely forgotten about an outfit. Richard must have seen the look of pure horror on her face as he continued,

"We require our girls to wear something sexy. You know lingerie and stuff. Most of the girls wear bikinis and heels. If you're stuck, there is a shop at the top of the hill that sells some good stuff."

Stacey thought about the pink bikini Lucia had made her buy.

"I think I have something. What time shall I start?"

"Normally we ask the girls to be here at ten, so if you want to grab your bits and head back here straight away I'll allow you to work late tonight, but only tonight. If you're not here by ten on any other night, you won't be allowed to work. OK?"

"Yes perfect. Thanks. I'll be back in ten minutes."

"Brilliant, see you soon. And, Stacey."

"Yes?"

"Make sure you cover that eye up. I don't want my girls looking like they've had a round with Mike Tyson."

Stacey felt the heat rise to her cheeks, she tried to think of a suitable reply but she could do no more than nod in Richard's direction. Even though she must look a right state, she was amazed that he had still decided to give her a chance. She headed back into the now chaotic streets of the West End with a spring in her step. Yes, she would have to dance naked but it would only be for a couple of nights then she could look for somewhere more suitable. That's when she saw him, the guy she'd caught watching her at Bora Bora. His gaze was concentrated on his phone and before she had a chance to confront him, he disappeared into the crowd; suddenly she was on high alert again and as she headed back to the hotel she watched over her shoulder, making sure he wasn't behind her. As hard as she was trying to stay out of trouble, it was starting to look like trouble was eventually going to find her.

3

Lucia's eyes widened as the black Jaguar, driven by Salvatore's driver, pulled up to the railed gates. The villa reminded her of an old gothic castle and as the gates slowly opened, she noticed that every detail had been accounted for, from the gargoyles who rested on the top of the roof, to the bronze lions who guarded the entrance. The gates shut behind them, making Lucia feel like she was entering a high security prison. Salvatore's driver took her case from the car and indicated for her to follow him as they walked to the front of the villa. The front door was made of a heavy-looking dark wood and Lucia waited with nervous anticipation as the driver reached for the bronze knocker which was carved into a smiling devil's face. *This place gives me the creeps*, Lucia thought as she waited to be let in. *But what choice do I have? I am completely stranded. I have little money saved and nowhere to stay.*

Entering the marble living room with its black grand piano, black leather seats, and big tropical plants, Lucia banished the horrible fight with Stacey to the back of her mind. As far as she was concerned, Stacey had abandoned her and Lucia had no time for her now.

She tried to block out all the negative thoughts that were building up in her mind. She'd been getting high for over twenty-four hours now and the scratching need for another line was starting to take over. As soon as the formalities were sorted with Salvatore, Lucia planned on indulging herself in his bathroom. In no way was her party going to be over now.

"Lucia, my love. So nice of you to call." Despite it being early morning and hot outside, Salvatore was wearing a black shirt and black suit trousers. Lucia's trained eye noticed that they were both Versace creations and from where she was standing, twenty yards away, she could smell his overpowering aftershave. She could also see that he was freshly shaven and his hair was neatly scraped into a ponytail. It was obvious that he'd made an effort. *Is it for me?* she wondered to herself, although deep down she already knew the answer. Her eyes fell upon the huge flowers he had arranged in vases around the room, the colour of them was such a dark red they almost looked black.

"You like my dahlias? I get them imported from Madrid. So exquisitely dark, so grotesque yet so beautiful. Just like life. Come here, let me look at you closer."

Unsure of what to do next, Lucia came closer. Salvatore took her chin in his hands and turned her face from side to side.

"Just like my dahlias, you really are exquisite. But you need cleaning up, taking care of."

Lucia remained quiet, her mind unable to focus on the words coming from his mouth.

"Why don't you sit down and relax whilst I get Romano to serve you a glass of champagne?"

On hearing those words, Lucia was content that she had come to the right place.

Somewhere she could chill, until she sorted herself out.

"Yes please, my darling. So kind."

"And some cocaine? There is some on that table over there. Just help yourself. My home is your home. OK?"

"If you're sure," Lucia said, as she walked over to the table, a thrill forming inside of her as she noticed the massive pile of cocaine that had been laid out. *She didn't have to be leaving so quickly*, she decided. *She had everything she needed right here.*

Salvatore's phone rang and he excused himself as he left her in the room.

"Did you see the other girl?" Salvatore asked in a hushed voice. "Well that's not good enough, she can't have just vanished. Check with that slut, see if she booked a taxi. For now, put Lucia's stuff in the spare room and get the maid to make the bed with the best sheets. And Alfonso? Watch her like a hawk. I do not want her to leave without my permission, under any circumstances. OK?" Salvatore put the phone down and watched as Lucia greedily sniffed two lines. She wouldn't be going anywhere as long as he kept the drugs coming, but without the other girl his plan couldn't come into action. He needed to find her and he needed to find her quickly.

4

Prodigy's *Smack My Bitch Up* was playing in Temptations and Stacey was dancing on stage as if her feet were on fire. She jumped onto the pole, using her soles to negotiate her way to the top. Suspended in mid-air, she looked down at all the punters gathered in the bar, wobbling slightly as her nerves got the better of her. She'd been working for two weeks now and to her surprise, she'd made over four hundred euros in her first night and even more on her second. It was only supposed to be temporary, the plan was to save enough for a week in a hotel whilst she looked for somewhere else to work, but when the money came in so thick and so fast, it seemed stupid for her not to save more. It was easy to see that if she worked hard enough, she would be able to set herself up back home and regain employment doing what she loved. The knowledge that she was working towards something gave her a new focus and she blanked out the idiots that came to the club, honing her sights on the shyer, geeky guys. Seeing how nervous they were in front of her, made it easy for her to be more confident. The attention and the praise she was receiving from the customers, along with the easy cash, was starting to become addictive.

When she stepped into the club, it was like she was entering a whole other world. She wasn't shy Stacey anymore, she was Amber – the sexual temptress who men would pay vast amounts of money just to adore.

Stacey's days with Lucia were starting to fade into a distant memory. She hadn't heard from her since their argument and she hadn't tried to contact her. All her life she had cared for the people she loved, but now she wanted to be as independent as possible. Which was just as well, as the only friends she had made since arriving in San Antonio were Richard and Matt. Most of the girls that she worked with were off their heads on something and after Lucia's drug taking she'd decided to keep her distance. She liked not having ties to anyone, it felt incredible to be so free and that's how she intended to keep it for now. Matt popped into the club every couple of days to see how she was doing and most evenings was her dinner companion, her treat of course. Whilst they chowed down on the best food in Ibiza, he would fill her in on all the goings on. Apparently, there was trouble on the island, stemming from a deal that had gone wrong at the opening of Space.

Stacey knew it had something to do with the drugs but she didn't react in front of Matt.

She'd made herself a new life in San Antonio and in no way did she want the trouble from before catching up with her. Not that she had much choice, a couple of times she'd spotted the man from Bora Bora in the back streets of the West End but now instead of wanting to confront him, she just ran for cover before he'd had a chance to spot her. She'd tried to convince herself that she was in the clear but deep down, she knew the danger hadn't disappeared yet. There would be some kind of retribution, of this she was sure. She just hoped that when it did kick off, Lucia and herself would be as far away from the island as possible.

The song reached its crescendo as Stacey spun upside down. She twisted to one side and pulled off her top. setting her breasts free as she hung there. She'd picked up all her tricks from watching the other girls dance. It was all about being able to lift your own body weight, something which she had found surprisingly easy to do. Loud cheers and wolf whistles filled the club and upside down, she allowed herself another glance into the audience. She nearly fell off the pole when she spotted him, *Aaron*. He was propped up against the bar facing the stage, his face was contorted in shock as she hung in the air, topless. She could feel her cheeks burning with shame. The song was still playing and her only choice was to carry on. All she wanted to do was run off the stage and preserve her dignity but she knew it was too late for that. Instinctively, she put her hands over her breasts. Some of the customers shouted at her but all she could think about was Aaron.

She could feel his eyes boring into her and forced herself to look in his direction. He was still standing in the same spot, his expression solemn and troubled. The song ended and she grabbed her clothes, hurrying to put them on as Richard came towards her, his face screwed up in confusion.

"Are you OK, Amber? You look like you've seen a ghost." She glanced over at Aaron who was still standing in the same spot as before.

"Is he bothering you? Do you want me to kick him out?"

"No it's OK. He's just a friend who didn't know I did this."

"Don't ever feel bad in front of a man for making money. You're a good girl, OK?"

Stacey nodded as Richard scuffed up her hair affectionately.

"Thanks for everything, Rich," she said, overcome by his show of concern.

"It's OK, as I said before you're a good 'un. Don't let anyone tell you otherwise."

Stacey tried to focus on what Richard was saying but Aaron's presence in her peripheral was proving too much of a distraction. She wanted to go over to speak to him but she was rooted to the spot. Ever since she had arrived at San Antonio, she'd been hiding away from Lucia, the drugs and herself. She knew that talking to him could bring it all back. *What would she even say to him?* It's not like she could tell him the truth about it all. His gaze felt like it was burning through her and, unable to ignore it any longer, she swallowed the lump in her throat and headed over to him.

"You keep getting more and more naked each time I see you, Stacey." His eyes had the same glint in them as when he'd seen her at Amnesia yet this time there was a touch of melancholy behind them.

"Nice to see you too," she said, sounding braver than she felt.

"I've been looking out for you in Amnesia. I didn't think in a million years you'd be working here. What's with the job change? I mean, no offence, but you are so much better than this." The music was echoing through Stacey's ears and she had to strain in order to hear Aaron as he spoke to her.

"Me? I was just about to ask you the same thing. Didn't think you were the strip club type." He glanced to the ground awkwardly, making Stacey feel bad for goading him.

"But if you must know, Aaron, I am saving to go home and start a new life for myself."

"Oh, OK, that's good. Look, I'm sorry for asking. I know it's none of my business. It's just a shock seeing you here. I've got to admit you're looking well though, babe." Aaron's eyes flicked up and down Stacey, making her instantly want to cover up.

"Well thank you for your concern. It's a shock to see you here too. I never thought you, of all people, would be here." Aaron looked around uncomfortably at her question.

"What do you mean me, of all people?"

"You really want me to spell it out?"

"Well yeah. I'd like to know what you think of me."

"You're a good looking guy Aaron, and obviously you're not short of a bob or two. Most of the guys that come here don't have a clue. You just don't seem like the type, that's all."

"Money ain't everything, but you're right, I don't usually come to these places.

For some reason I felt drawn here and if I'm honest I'm glad that I came." He smiled at Stacey for a brief second then his eyes scanned the room. "Look, babe, I need to talk to you about the other night. Will you come with me to the private room? I think we can discuss things better there."

Stacey couldn't help a smile from forming on her face.

"You want to take me upstairs, *to talk*?"

"It's so hard to believe?"

The last thing Stacey wanted to do was to dance for Aaron, but the sincerity in his brown eyes reassured her that he was telling the truth. Without saying another word, she held out her hand, and signalled for him to follow her upstairs.

Aaron wouldn't lift his eyes up from the ground as they entered the private room and even Stacey found herself looking nervously around her.

"Here we are," she said, closing the opaque curtain behind them. Without looking up from the ground, Aaron pulled out a wad of cash from his pocket and tried to hand it to her.

"What are you doing? Put that away!" She shut the curtain behind her as Aaron reached into his pocket, pulling out a wad of cash that Stacey estimated to be well over three hundred euros.

"You are worth so much more than that, Stacey. Look, I know you don't want to be doing this, so just take it, please." He made eye contact with her as he pushed the money into Stacey's hands. "Put it in your bag and don't think anything of it."

"I can't take this," Stacey said, holding the money limply in her hands.

"Yes you can and you will. Put it towards your flight out of here."

Stacey passed the cash back to Aaron who reached towards her bag and started to shove it inside.

"What are you doing?"

"Stacey for God's sake I'm trying to help you."

"I don't need your help."

"Really? So you're doing this job for fun?"

"Who do you think you are? Coming here and judging me."

"I'm not judging you. I care about you, that's all." He pushed the last of the money into her bag as she held back the tears which had now gathered in her eyes.

"Thank you." She kissed him on the cheek, lingering a bit longer than she wanted to.

"You're incredible," he said as she pulled away.

"You really didn't have to do this."

"But I wanted to," Aaron said as he sat down on the foldable chair his frame almost dominating the seat. "Are you gonna come and join me?" He indicated the space on his lap.

"I can't, it's against the rules."

"I've already told you. I don't want to do anything dodgy. I just want you to sit close to me so I can talk to you. You won't be able to hear anything if you stand there."

Stacey hesitated, the awkwardness of the situation making it impossible to put herself in a good light. Taking a deep breath, she placed herself on top of him, her body instantly heating up as it touched his own.

"That's better, God you smell so good."

"So what was it you wanted to speak to me about?" Stacey asked, trying to dispel the sexual tension that was rising between them. Aaron let out a deep sigh, his breath sending quivers down Stacey's spine.

"First of all, I wanted to apologize for the other night. I should have believed you when you said you didn't know that guy. I never should have spoken to you the way I did."

"I'm not going to lie, you were rude. I really didn't know him but he is a friend of Lucia's."

"She knows him?"

"Well yeah, he is a friend of her ex-boyfriend. What I don't get is how you know him?"

"Is she here tonight?"

"No, we fell out a couple of weeks ago. Hence me being here. Are you going to answer my question?"

"You fell out? What happened?"

"Stop avoiding my questions, Aaron. I'm not going to say another word till you tell me what's going on."

"Look, things are complicated with me right now and if I tell you stuff it could do more harm than good. All I can say is that I'm glad you're not associated with him. I know a lot about the people who work on this island and most of them would sell their own mother to make a profit. Let's just say he isn't one of the good guys."

"So Lucia could be in danger?"

"If she's stupid enough to be with him, then yes."

"You're being serious?"

"With him anything is possible."

"So she's in trouble? For fuck's sake! I need to get her away from him. She wasn't in a good place. I shouldn't have left her." Stacey put her head in her hands and unable to control her emotions any longer started to sob.

"Don't cry, Stacey. I didn't mean to upset you. I'm sure your friend is OK, come on." He pulled her towards him, lifted her head and wiped the tears from her eyes. Stacey realised he was going to kiss her; it was against the rules of the club yet she didn't want to stop him. He reached over to her, his lips brushing against her own. She felt electrified as he massaged her tongue delicately with his. It took all her willpower to pull away from him.

"I can't do this, not here."

"Please come with me. I can help you."

"I can't just leave."

"How much is it that you need?" Balancing her on his lap, he reached inside his back pocket and pulled another wad of cash out.

"For God's sake this isn't about money. What is it with you and thinking you can pay me off?"

"I just want to help you," he answered, looking completely grief stricken by her refusal.

"Why?"

"'Cause I like you, Stacey. Stop over thinking it."

"Look, Aaron, as much as I appreciate your generosity, I can't just take this to leave work, it's not right."

"Well let me help you with your friend at least."

The idea of telling Aaron about the drugs flashed through her thoughts but Stacey instantly dismissed it; she didn't want anything to jeopardize Lucia's safe return.

"I'm not paying you to leave with me, Stacey. I know that's what it looks like but I'm not. I wanna be there for you and yes, I want you out of here. The two things come hand in hand. Tell your manager you're ill or something. Give me one night to explain things.

"*Please*. I'm not talking sex. You need to know what Ibiza is really about before you decide to go and rescue your friend."

Stacey sat on Aaron's lap, not knowing what to do or to say, her hands still full with his money.

"Here, take this." She passed the cash back to him, feeling instantly relieved in doing so.

"Up." He gently pushed her off him and went over to her bag, placing the rest of the cash inside.

"Aaron, stop!"

"No I won't. I don't want you here. What's more if you are serious about your friend you have to come with me. I'm the only one who can help you." He leant into her and gave her a slow, lingering kiss. Once again she

187

pulled away, afraid that she would lose herself in the moment.

"Of course I am serious. I owe her everything. She took me away from my life and gave me opportunities I could only dream of. I never should have left her."

"I will do all I can, babe, but please, let's just get out of here. I can't see you here any longer."

"OK, OK, you win. I'll speak to Richard." Stacey's head was so muddled that as she grabbed her bag and headed out the room, she didn't even know whether she was doing the right thing anymore.

"Why do you want to leave? It's busy tonight, you can make a fortune if you stay." The disappointment was evident in Richard's voice as he stared at her quizzically.

"It's just as I said, he is an old friend and I don't know when I am going to see him again."

"Don't let this man throw you off track, you're doing really well so far and you've nearly got enough to go home. Remember your plans, kiddo."

"I know, I know but I have to do this. I'll call you tomorrow, OK?"

"Make sure you do. Something about this isn't right, Stacey. I'm sure I recognize his face and for some reason it's not a good memory. Any trouble, give me a bell."

"Thanks, Rich. I don't know what I would do without you." Stacey gave him a tip out of Aaron's money.

"Where the hell did you get all that?" Richard asked handing it back to her.

"He gave it to me. Please just take it."

"I don't need your money, hon, especially from men like him. You know whatever you're getting yourself into be careful. I've seen hundreds of good girls like you get sucked in by these gangster types. Their cash can't buy your safety though, remember that."

"He's not a gangster," Stacey answered, the uncertainty in her voice undeniable to even her own ears.

"And I'm a bloody priest. Open your eyes, Stacey, he's got it written all over him."

"I'll be fine," Stacey said, angry that Richard might actually be right about Aaron.

"Don't say I didn't warn you pet."

Stacey tried to erase Richard's words from her head as she slipped into her denim shorts, silver boob tube and black wedges. She reached for her mobile, her hands shook as she dialled Lucia's number. *Would she even want to speak to her?* The phone went to straight to an automated Spanish voice. Stacey couldn't tell whether it was voicemail or a message to say the number was no longer in use. There was no beep after the message and Stacey felt a sinking feeling in her stomach. *What if something had already happened to her?* She grabbed her stuff and headed towards the exit. Aaron was waiting by the door, his face appeared shocked yet happy as she approached. To the left of him, too close not to be an acquaintance, was an older man who had to be as wide as he was tall.

"I take it you managed to get off then?" Aaron asked her, the cheeky look back on his face.

"Yeah, you're very lucky. My manager didn't want to let me go," Stacey answered, her eyes falling over the man who was now glaring at her.

"This is my mate, Stan." The huge man, who looked like a bear, didn't change his stern expression as he held out his hand.

"Good to meet you," Stan said, his gravelly voice sounding as if he'd been dragged up in the East End of London.

"Yes you too," she said, suddenly becoming nervous at the thought of spending the night with Aaron and his hulk of a friend. She watched nervously as Stan turned away from her and started speaking to Aaron in his ear.

"Nice to meet you, Stace," he said, turning back to face her. He patted Aaron on the back before scanning the area and walking out the doors.

"Thank God he's got the hint and done one." Aaron laughed nervously as he reached for Stacey's hand. "Come on, let's get outta here."

Stacey had no choice but to submit to him. Not only was his body magnetizing her with such a force that she couldn't pull away, but more importantly he was the key to rescuing her best friend whose welfare she had neglected for far too long. All the loud music, bright lights and intoxicated tourists faded into the background as she took Aaron's hand and followed him into the heat of the Ibizan night: praying in the back of her mind that she wasn't too late to save Lucia.

5

Aaron's bike zoomed along the coastal road of San Antonio, causing Stacey's hair to whip frantically across her face. She pressed into his shoulders, shielding herself from the wind as they turned into a side road. The terrain beneath them was a lot bumpier now and she held onto Aaron even tighter, scared that she would be flung off. There were no streetlights and as they pulled into another smaller road, Aaron's bike skidded across the sand beneath. He parked next to a weathered restaurant, the full moon illuminating the enclosed beach in front of them. His hands were on Stacey's body as helped her off the bike, the sound of the engine replaced by the waves colliding against the shore.

"I'm sorry if it was a bit rough back there and for bringing you out this far. I just wanted to get away from San An, it's full of wrong un's this time of night."

"It's OK, this beats the noise and all those bright lights anytime." She turned to Aaron who had sat himself down in front of the sea, his hands playing with the sand distractedly. "So, did you mean it when you said you could help rescue Lucia?"

"I give you my word, Stace." Aaron answered his eyes locking into her own. "Come, sit down." He indicated to the spot next him. "I really do love this beach. Sometimes, when things get too much, I come and just watch the waves."

"Too much? You seem like you have it all."

"As they say, appearances can be deceptive."

"So tell me something about it."

"I will, I promise and you'll probably run a mile afterwards but first, let's sort this situation out with your mate. You said something to me before about her rescuing you from your life back home. What did you mean by that, Stace?"

Stacey let out a deep sigh, wondering how much she could truly reveal.

"Lucia did more than just rescue me, she helped me become something I could only dream of being. Ever since I met her she's had this unrelenting faith in me. She's my best friend and I owe her my life."

"So Lucia isn't the type of girl to be involved in something behind your back like?"

"No way. What makes you say that?"

"I need to know if she's on our side."

"Of course she is, she didn't even like that creep before she took that stuff. The only reason she went with him was 'cause she was completely spangled and wasn't seeing things clearly."

"So what you really trying to say, is she might not leave if she is still under the influence?"

"No, well, to be honest, I don't know. But that doesn't mean I can just give up on her. Would you give up on someone you loved?"

"No, of course not but Salvatore has a way of manipulating people. We're going to have to bide our time, whilst I make some enquiries."

"Great. So I've got to sit back whilst she is with someone who could potentially be harming her?"

"We can't just go marching in, Stace, especially when your friend has decided to play with a fucking deadly snake like him. Believe me, I know what it's like to feel helpless."

Stacey remembered the night at Amnesia when she'd first noticed the pain behind Aaron's confident stance.

"Why are you here Aaron? And don't lie to me about partying. I can see it's something deeper than that."

Stacey watched as Aaron shifted uncomfortably in the sand, the dark waves crashing in his brown eyes.

"It's my brother. He's gotten himself in a lot of trouble here. He owes money to some very dangerous people. But the problem is he's so fucking delusional,

194

the divvy actually believes he's invincible. Of course he's not and the truth of it all is it's about to seriously catch up with him. The worse part, he's an addict. He's on the heavy stuff and therefore not mentally equipped to handle the hole he's dug himself into."

Stacey felt her stomach contract like she'd just been punched in her gut. She couldn't believe that Aaron, much like herself, knew the agonizing duty you felt towards a family member entrapped by drugs.

"Are you OK, Stace? You've gone real quiet on me love. I'm sorry if it's all too much for you."

"No, please don't think that. The only reason I've gone quiet is 'cause I can totally relate to it. The amount of times I've had to fight my mum's battles for her,"

"Your mum has a drug problem?"

"Yep. I've tried and I've tried but in the end it all got too much and I had to leave her to fend for herself. Who knows what will happen to her now I've gone? She'll probably be found dead in a squat somewhere." Stacey rubbed away the tears which had started to roll down her face. Aaron reached out towards her, cradling her head between his arms.

"Oh, babe, I know how you feel. Please don't be upset. There's nothing you can do about it now. You have to live your life." He pulled her away from him and softly wiped the tears from her face. "I can't believe how wrong I was about you. I thought you were this sheltered girl from London. I didn't even realise how similar our lives were. Come on don't cry, you're way, way too pretty."

"That's what you said to me before in Space." Stacey said forcing herself to smile.

"I meant it then, the same as I mean it now. A girl like you should never be anything but happy."

"You sound like Lucia, she was always telling me how life is meant to be this joyous thing, and with her it usually was. I wish to God things hadn't gotten so bad between us."

"What did you two row about, if you don't mind me asking? I don't want to make you upset again, so if you don't want to tell me."

"No, it's fine. As you know she was so off her face at work she nearly got us both fired. Then when we got back to our apartment our deranged landlady decided to kick us out. I thought the idea of us being homeless would bring Lucia round but she still wouldn't stop taking coke so I poured her stuff down the sink. She was so mad, she went for me. It was horrible, I didn't want to leave her but I couldn't stay, especially when she wanted us to go to Salvatore's."

"Sounds like you did the right thing leaving when you did."

For a moment, Stacey considered telling Aaron about the drugs but she instantly dismissed the idea. After all, they were probably back with their right owner now and there was no point in bringing unnecessary complications to what was an already stressful situation.

"After I saw you in Temptations, I tried to ring her phone but it was off. If anything has happened to her, I'll never forgive myself. I should have never let her go to him."

"You shouldn't blame yourself, Stace. Ibiza isn't all sunsets and partying. There's a dark side and unfortunately Lucia has decided to bunk up with the Lord of Darkness himself. Luckily for her I have someone on the inside who will tell me if she's still there, what her mental state is like and whether she'll put up a fight if we try to rescue her. Whilst this is going on, I need to know you're somewhere he can't reach you. He won't think twice about hunting you down. Especially if he knows about us."

"Us?"

"I don't go around just kissing any girls I meet, Stace and your association with me could lead you into a lot of trouble."

"Why?"

"'Cause of who I represent whilst I'm here."

"What do you mean?"

Aaron buried his face in his hand and let out a deep sigh.

"You remember, Stan?"

"Course I do."

"Well Stan's been my minder since I was born."

"Minder? Why?"

"Because of my dad. He's well known in the criminal world and being his son makes me a prime target to his enemies. My dad owns a lot of the turf out here, places Salvatore is desperate to get his greasy little hands on. I know he was also responsible for having my villa robbed at gun point last year.

"One of his men shot my friend in the leg, causing her to be wheelchair bound for the rest of her life. It wasn't an accident either, he planned it that way. This island is like the Wild West at the moment. Any day now it's all about to seriously kick off and I don't want you to be here when it does. That's why you need to go back to London, wait for your friend and forget all about me."

"Why would I want to forget you?" Stacey got up and started to walk towards the sea.

"Where are you doing?"

"I can't listen to this anymore. I'm going swimming."

"Stacey, wait, come back here. I'm not finished."

Stacey pulled off her top and shorts and ran towards the sea. Not knowing whether she was running into her problems, or away from them as the water hit her bare ankles. She was paddling in the water by the time Aaron had caught up with her; he grabbed around her waist as he spun her around to meet him. He leant into her, his

wet chest sliding against her own as his lips. met hers...
They kissed with such a raw intensity Stacey felt herself
becoming lost in the moment. Needing to regain her
composure, she pulled away from him and immersed
herself under the water. Holding her breath, Stacey
floated above the sea bed and allowed the cold water to
invigorate her follicles. She resurfaced, flicking her wet
hair away from her face. Aaron was looking at her with
an intensity in his eyes, droplets of water slowly
trickling down his chest. He glided towards her, his
hands reaching around her waist as he pressed his nose
and forehead against her own.

"You have to believe me when I say that I couldn't
live with myself if anything happened to you because of
me." He kissed her softly, then paused keeping his face
still close to her own. Stacey let out a deep sigh; she'd
never felt as calm and as frustrated as she did in that
moment.

"I don't understand, if you hate your life so much
why don't you just try to go incognito and do something
else? Surely your parents would understand and help
you?"

"You don't know my parents. Now I've met you, I
wish more than anything that I was just on holiday
without a care in the world but it's not that easy. There is
a lot of shit I need to sort out on this island. A lot of
scores that need settling and it's not going to be pretty. I
really like you Stacey, but as I said I couldn't bear it if
something happened to you because of me."

Aaron turned his gaze to the horizon which was now becoming brighter with the first rays of the sun.

"Come on. Let's get you back."

Teeth chattering, Stacey leant into Aaron and pressed her lips against his. She wanted to tell him that it didn't matter about the danger, that she had already fallen for him but she knew she'd just sound crazy. Instead, she kissed him even harder as the pink sunrise of the night welcomed in the vivid blue sky of the day.

Without any sleep or rest, Stacey should have felt exhausted but as Aaron followed her upstairs, all she could feel was excitement. The room was sticky with the heat as Stacey entered. Aaron stood at the door, his eyes boring into her. She motioned for him to come inside and he shut the door cautiously behind him, as she pulled down the blinds and turned on the air-con.

Aaron strode towards her, lifting her off the ground, he made her squeal with surprise. He spun her around and placed her on the bed, then started to take off her shorts. Stacey knew the right thing to do would be to make him wait, act a bit coy but she wanted him so bad, she couldn't resist. It felt so right to have his mouth move from her ankles all the way to her neck. He started to undress himself in front of her and instinctively she reached out across his body, feeling the contrast of his soft skin against his hard, protruding muscles. They were now both naked and he pulled away from her, staring at her body for what felt like an eternity.

"You're so beautiful," Aaron whispered, almost breathlessly as his fingers followed the outline of her breasts. She smiled, allowing his hands to move around her body. He pushed her hair behind her ear and kissed her neck. There was no turning back now, she wanted this man like she had never wanted anyone before. His kisses glided down onto her torso, till his lips arrived between her legs. She groaned as his tongue explored her wetness, her body pulsating against his mouth. Stacey could taste herself on his lips as they rejoined her own, and surrendered into him as he slowly pushed himself inside her. She felt herself become electrified as he thrust himself between her legs. It was a sensation that lifted her higher than she had ever been before, till eventually she felt like she had transcended from her own body. It was only after two hours of making love, breathless and dripping with sweat, that they stopped, both completely exhausted.

"You are the most amazing girl."

Stacey didn't have the energy to even answer back as Aaron got up, his perfect bare bum on display. She watched as he suddenly stopped in his tracks, his focus now on the hat she'd unwittingly stolen from Space that was positioned on top of her suitcase.

"It's you," he muttered almost incomprehensibly. "The girl from the CCTV."

Stacey was still enjoying the feeling that his body had given her but as she registered the serious tone to Aaron's voice, she forced herself to sit up.

"What are you talking about?"

"They're looking for you and your friend. The girls who took the drugs." Stacey bit down on her lip and tried to think but nothing came to her mind. "Tell me I'm wrong, please, Stace."

"I wish I could," she said, sighing.

"So it was *you*?"

"We didn't take them. They were put in my bag. I didn't want any part of it!"

"And you expect me to believe that? Why didn't you tell me? And who do you mean by 'we'?"

"Lucia and I. You have to believe me, Aaron, we didn't and still don't have a clue who they belonged to, or why they ended up in my bag. I didn't tell you because I thought it was all over and I didn't want to go dragging it all up again."

"What do you mean, you thought it was all over?" Aaron started to pace the room with her hat in his hand. Stacey had never seen him look so angry, and part of her actually felt nervous around the man she'd just made passionate love with. Suddenly feeling very naked she reached for the bed sheet and wrapped it around her body.

"They were taken from us. We don't know how; our room was locked. We'd tried to give them back, but the only person we knew to go to was Tomas."

"Tomas, the security guard at Space?"

"Yes, you know him?"

"Yes, of course I do. I never thought he would be stupid enough to take the drugs, but since no one has been able to locate him and he is clearly seen handing you girls the bag containing the drugs on camera, everyone assumed he was guilty."

"How did they know the drugs were in my bag?"

"The Guardia were on their way to bust someone and the coke was stashed in there.

"Before there was a chance for it to be retrieved, the bag was taken by Tomas and given to you."

"Well, wasn't it obvious that it was just a mistake?"

"Not after Tomas went missing and then you girls."

"But we tried to give them back! Then when they were taken from us, we just assumed and hoped, they'd been taken by the rightful owner."

"And you swear you're telling me the truth?"

"I swear, Aaron! You think I would be working at Temptations if I had been involved in stealing that amount of cocaine? It must be worth about fifty grand."

"I believe you, Stace, but you should have told me. I could have sorted it out."

"I'm sorry but I didn't want you to get involved."

"Well I am involved and I need to know everything. Starting with their disappearance. Where and when did they go missing?"

"How are you involved? Are they your drugs, Aaron?"

"No, but I've been put in the frame for them being taken. Now, please just tell me what happened. We haven't got time to waste."

"OK, OK. They were taken from our room the night I saw you at Amnesia. Before we realised they were missing, Lucia was intent on getting Salvatore to help us with them, but your warning kept ringing through my head and I wouldn't let her call him. As far as I know she hadn't told him about the drugs, but I can't be sure."

"Where were you staying when they were taken?"

"Some weird hostel in Figueretas. The owner chucked us out, minutes after we found them missing. She claimed she'd seen two men in our apartment that night. I don't know whether she was lying to us or what, but there is no way someone could have just let themselves in.

"Then Lucia and I came to blows and I left her to go to San Antonio. I promise you we had nothing to do with any of it." Stacey could feel herself start to hyperventilate but she knew it was imperative that she explain herself as well as she could, so she forced herself to continue.

"If someone *did* break into our room, it wouldn't be the first time. We had to leave our apartment in San Antonio 'cause someone broke in, although that time they didn't find the drugs. I think it's this guy, who I'm sure has been following us. He was watching me on

204

Bora Bora beach and then I saw him again in the West End"

"It's definitely a possibility, the drugs are still classed as missing and there's a ton of cash on both your heads. The image on the CCTV was pretty distorted though, you can only see the back of Lucia and your face is covered by that hat"

"Do you think Salvatore knows it's her?"

"It's possible."

"Right, that's it. I've got to get her out of there now, Aaron. What if he's hurt her? I can't let anything happen to her."

"Let me sort this, Stace, all you need to concentrate on is getting back home."

Stacey registered Aaron telling her to go home and it made her feel sick to her stomach. *How could she go back when everything that was important to her was in Ibiza Bizz?*

"What about this guy, the one who's been following me? I bet he's got something to do with all of this. He'd be easy to find, he's not like any of the other tourists. He's probably one of the palest guys I've seen since I've been here, he's always hiding behind these black Ray bans and he has this skull tattoo."

"On his neck. For fuck's sake!"

"You know him?"

"I don't just know him."

"What do you mean?"

"That's my fucking brother." Aaron sank onto the bed, his head in his hands.

"Your brother?"

"Yeah, and the man whose drugs everyone is looking for."

The room went silent, Stacey didn't know what else to say. Aaron wasn't moving from his position. Then, out of nowhere, he got up and kicked the wall with such force she was sure it was going to cave in.

"I'm sorry. One day, when I have time on my side, I will explain to you the whole story of my brother. I've really got to find him before he does any more damage. When was the last time you saw him?"

"A couple of days ago, just off the West End."

"How quick can you get your stuff packed? I've got a mate at the airport; he can get you on the next flight back to London but you've got to be ready to go soon as."

"You really want me to go?"

"What I want is for you to be safe and you're not when you're here."

"I've done OK so far. Plus, I've got you to look after me now."

"I haven't got time for this. Come on, get your bag ready."

"I'm not going back, Aaron. Lucia needs me here."

"What are you going to do? Rescue her yourself? This isn't a game. These are real men with real guns who don't care who they hurt."

Stacey started to feel annoyed, *who did Aaron think he was, ordering her about?*

"I know this isn't a game. This is my friend and I'm not leaving her. Now if you don't mind I need to get some sleep."

"Why are you acting like a child? Do you wanna be killed on this island? Because you're going the right way about it." He tried to lift her off the bed but she pulled away from him.

"Get off me! I'm staying here and nothing you can say or do will make me change my mind. Either accept my decision or just leave me alone!"

She knew she'd taken it too far by the look in Aaron's eyes, yet she couldn't bring herself to call him back as he stormed out of her room, slamming the door behind him. The silence suddenly felt suffocating to her as she realised that like she'd stupidly requested, she was once again, all alone. She rolled herself into a ball on her bed and cried till she found herself drifting off. She welcomed the sleep as it fell upon her, grateful for its ability to wipe away her worries and fears, even if the relief was only temporary.

The Come Down

1

The lights of the West End blinded Stacey as she stepped outside her hotel. Her head was pounding; she'd never slept in this late before and was surprised to see it was nightfall already. She tried to remember what time she'd gone to bed but everything was a blur. The only thing she could remember vividly was Richard telling her not to come back to work until she sorted herself out.

It had been three days since her encounter with Aaron and she still hadn't heard from him. She'd tried to pretend she wasn't bothered but going by the amount of alcohol she had consumed over the last two nights, she knew her heart was slowly breaking with his rejection. She couldn't figure out whether it was his intention to use her all along, or whether he was just still angry with her. Either way, all she wanted to do was numb the pain she felt.

Stacey had tried to ring Lucia on numerous occasions, but as always, her phone went straight to voicemail. The thought that something terrible had happened to Lucia haunted Stacey. She felt frustrated and completely helpless and with no word from Aaron, she hadn't a clue how she could bring her friend back to safety.

Richard had warned Stacey to go easy on the drink but she hadn't listened. She knew he was upset and disappointed but it was like she didn't care about anything anymore.

With everyone who had mattered now gone from her life, there was nothing else for her to do but drown her sorrows.

Stacey adjusted herself to the bright lights and loud music and headed straight for the Irish bar, opposite her hotel. Every night an annoyingly chirpy Irish guy called Dermot would beckon, and then plead with her to come in for a free drink, and every night, she would explain that she had work. Not tonight, tonight she was ready to party; sitting herself down, she called a shocked-looking Dermot over to her.

"Wow! I thought you would never join us! You look grand! I take it you're not working tonight?"

"No, for once I am not working, so you best be prepared to get me as pissed as possible."

"Good girl. We are going to party the Irish way!"

"Bring it on," Stacey said, ordering a double vodka and red bull.

2

"So you want to come out with us? We're going Hed Kandi at Pacha tonight and I could probably get you in for free if you want?"

Stacey took in the guy from Newcastle who not ten minutes previous had decided to plonk himself down next to her without an invitation. His over-gelled hair was styled in a short Mohican with not a strand out of place and his eyebrows were so neat and tidy it was obvious that they were maintained on a regular basis. His skin was a suspicious shade of orange, the type that screamed regular sunbed sessions, but what Stacey couldn't draw her eyes away from was his body. His muscles were way too big for his frame and his neck was literally non-existent. She suspected it was all due to steroid abuse, not that she was overly bothered, he was no Aaron but the way Stacey was feeling, she was happy for any attention she could get.

"Sounds good to me," Stacey answered, belching as she downed her fifth double vodka and red bull.

"We're jumping in the Suzuki soon. First, we need to go up town to sort out some party bits. You up for it?"

"Yeah course," Stacey answered, her head swaying from side to side.

"Mint pet. I'll let me mate know. You might have to sit on my lap though, if that's OK?"

"Perfect," Stacey replied, hiccupping as she did so.

Half an hour later, Stacey was sitting on the guy's, whose name she had forgotten, lap heading down the main road towards Ibiza Town. The guy had spent the whole journey with his hands on her legs and hips, and having drunk copious amounts of red bull and vodka, Stacey had found herself unable to push him away. She breathed a sigh of relief when the jeep pulled up outside Ave Espayna in Ibiza Town and she was told they were getting out.

"Are you coming with me?" the guy, whose name she'd just remembered was Anthony, asked, as he offered her his hand.

"Yeah sure. I'll come with you," Stacey responded, not wanting to be left with his mates.

Anthony led her up the cobbled backstreets of Ibiza Town till they reached a restaurant tucked away at the back. Within minutes, a scrawny looking guy with a mullet and denim waistcoat came up to them, his eyes shifting from side to side.

"What are you wanting?" he asked, his face not breaking into a smile.

Anthony told him the order and the man with the mullet informed him to wait where he was and order a drink. Without asking her what she wanted, Anthony ordered Stacey a Hierbas and coke, declaring it was the 'Drink of Ibiza'. Stacey didn't really like the taste of it but she was thirsty and it was cold, so she drank it without moaning.

"So you going to stay in my bed tonight, pet?" Anthony asked, his hands stroking her legs. Stacey's vision was blurred, she didn't even know if she'd make it through the night, let alone whether she would end up in this guy's bed. She was saved from answering by the denim-clad dealer, as he handed Anthony and herself a package each. Stacey turned the soft and powdery bag over in her hands. Even in her fuddled mind, it was obvious he'd just received a large amount of cocaine. She knew that sniffing a line would probably sober her up, and suddenly she felt more hopeful that she would be at least able to last the night without passing out in a drunken stupor.

It all seemed to happen so fast; one minute Anthony and Stacey were walking along the road, the next thing she saw two cars with *Guardia Civil* written on them parked next to the jeep. She became aware, even in her drunken stupor, that if she tried to turn around and walk off it would look suspicious, so she carried on walking. Not that it stopped Anthony, he simply legged it as fast as he could down the street. This sparked the interest of the Guardia, who grabbed her and chased after Anthony. Stacey's thoughts immediately turned to the cocaine in her bag. She could see the other lads lined up against the jeep, obviously them parking in a no parking zone with their hazards on had caught the Guardia's attention. The uniformed men started to search her bag, it didn't take them long to find the cocaine. The officer who'd discovered it pulled it out into the air so all the others could see, whilst another one placed some metal handcuffs on her. As Stacey was escorted to a barred car, she couldn't bring herself to feel any emotion but shock. She'd just been caught with a shit load of cocaine on her and the realisation that she was now in a lot of trouble was too much for her to bear.

3

Stacey was dragged out of the barred car, her hands forced as far behind her as they would go. She tried to plead with the two officers who had driven her to the station but they completely ignored her. They marched her inside the reception of the *Policia Nacional Station,* laughing with each other, like it was one big joke. She'd tried to be brave, but she couldn't stop the tears streaming uncontrollably from her eyes as they took her into custody. The man behind the desk had huge bags underneath his eyes and merely glanced at her, as the officers spoke to him in what she assumed was Spanish. She tried to think of a legitimate reason for the drugs being on her, but her thoughts were still muddled from the alcohol. She didn't have a clue how much cocaine was in the bag but she was guessing by the size of it that it must've been about five grams. All she could think about was how many years in prison that would get her. She had to face facts, she was looking at a custodial sentence for that amount. Still in handcuffs, she was led more gently to a corridor by another officer and ordered to wait against a wall. Through the glass doors at the other end of the passage, she could see some of the Newcastle lads waiting in a separate area. They were all handcuffed, their faces looking solemn yet defiant. She tried to look for Anthony but he wasn't amongst his friends, and she wondered if he'd actually managed to get away.

A different officer turned up and escorted her to a big cell-like room where two women in blue uniforms were waiting. The officer took off Stacey's cuffs and she wriggled the circulation back into her hands as the two women came either side of her.

"Please take off all your clothes and then squat on the floor."

It was the first time someone had properly addressed her in English, yet she wished she didn't understand the meaning. In no way did she want to take her clothes off in front of these strangers, let alone squat.

"I will not ask you again. Please take off your clothes and then squat down to the floor."

Stacey wanted to protest but she knew that she would eventually have to comply. She felt a shame rush over her body, as she peeled off her black dress and stood in front of the female officers naked. At that moment she longed to be back with her mum, or fighting with Lucia, anything had to be better than this.

"Now squat please."

Stacey crouched down feebly, which only seemed to anger the dark-haired woman standing in front of her even more.

"Lower. Do not waste our time," the woman demanded as she pressed her hand down onto Stacey's shoulders.

Stacey squatted down on the floor as low she could manage; her whole body was shaking from crying.

"OK. We are finished. Get dressed now."

Still sobbing, Stacey got dressed, was re-cuffed and then taken down some stairs. The stairs led to a basement jail, with several rooms. Amongst the shadows, Stacey could just make out the outline of the other prisoners. Her body started to convulse as she was led to one of the empty cells, the full extent of what was about to happen to her finally sinking in. The cell she was taken to was completely dark but she could just make out a small puddle in it, from the light outside. The guard pushed her inside as she screamed out in protest.

"*Buenos Noches*,"He whispered, locking the door behind her.

4

The key turning in the metal lock woke Stacey from her sleep. She shuddered as she saw a cockroach crawl across the stone floor past her bed. A guard with a stern and unshaved face called for her to come out. The after effects of the alcohol meant her head was throbbing, and her mouth had gone completely dry but she didn't waste any time.

Pulling herself off the waterproof mattress, she followed the guard up the stairs to where she'd been taken in the night before.

"What's happening now?" she asked the guard, whose face remained blank.

He took her to a chair and told her to wait. She felt like she hadn't washed in a year, her whole body was itchy. On closer inspection, she could see her legs and arms were covered in mosquito bites. She desperately needed some water but was suddenly consumed with a greater urge to urinate. At the far end of the cubicle she spotted a guard.

She got up and started to walk towards him; seeing her move, he started striding towards her, truncheon in hand. He was an older guy with grey hair and moustache. She could see that he had a much more sympathetic look to him than the previous guards.

"Que?" He asked her in a tone which she took to mean 'what?'

"Toilet please and water."

The guard looked around nervously, then taking her handcuffed arms, took her through another corridor to some sterile-looking toilets. He indicated for her to go in and pointed to the spot where he would be waiting. As she walked towards the mirrors the first thing that hit her was her reflection. She inwardly gasped as she noticed her eyelid had expanded painfully over her eye. *You look like bloody Quasimodo!* she thought to herself, not knowing whether to laugh or cry. It was obvious a mosquito had feasted on her eyelid whilst in she was in that filthy cell. She ran hot water over her grubby and tear-stained face, which made her feel slightly more human. She heard a female voice and there was knock on the door. Stacey rushed to the toilet and when she came out she saw a female guard waiting outside with a cup of water in her hand. Her face dropped as she caught sight of Stacey's appearance. She passed Stacey the water, and escorted her to an office just past the corridor, where a man wearing a grey suit sat waiting for her at a dark, wooden desk.

"Welcome, Stacey. My name is Diego, Constapolis. Please be seated."

Stacey's heart quickened in her chest as she realised she would now be under examination. The guard left them, and Diego started sorting through the papers in front of him. Stacey reluctantly sat down on the chair, her whole body starting to tremble as she did so.

"I'm right in saying, your full name is Stacey Michelle Mears?" Diego asked, his black, bushy, eyebrows almost meeting in the middle as he examined her passport.

"How the hell did you get that?" Stacey asked, as she stared at her passport in shock.

"We searched your room at the Don Juan. Now, will you confirm your name, please."

Stacey was stunned into silence, she never for a moment considered that they would know who she was, let alone find out where she lived.

"Yeah, that's me. How did you find my room?"

"One of your friends told us who you are."

Stacey tried to remember what she'd said to the Newcastle guys, but her memory was drawing blanks.

"I need to make you aware that the Don Juan, on light of this situation, have decided to evict you from their premises."

220

"What? What about my stuff? And my money?"

"You don't need to worry about this for now. Your belongings are safe and will be kept here until you are processed."

"What do you mean, *safe*?"

"They have been put in our care."

"What about my money, I suppose you're keeping that safe, too?"

"You were caught with a large quantity of drugs; any money found will have been confiscated until your trial."

"*Trial*?"

"Yes, of course you will have a trail. You have committed a serious crime and you could face prison. In order for us to process you and find a representation suitable for your case, you must now answer my questions. Do you understand?"

Stacey took a deep breath and nodded, deflated by her new situation.

"I understand you were taken in last night?"

"Yeah, last night," Stacey replied, as Diego wrote on a piece of paper pinned to a clipboard.

"And you were found to be in possession of a bag with over five grams of cocaine in it?"

Stacey tried to think clearly before answering, her heart was beating so fast she was sure Diego could hear it.

"Look, you said something about a representative. Well, I'd like to order that now if that's alright?"

"Yes it's your right as an EU citizen. We are currently waiting for a suitable one but these are *just* preliminary questions. You don't have to answer them but it will help to speed things up if you do."

"As much as I appreciate that you want to speed things up, I want to make sure I don't get fucked over, so until you can find me a suitable representative, I won't be answering any questions."

There was a long pause as Jorge removed his glasses and put his clipboard down.

Rubbing his eyes, he turned his gaze towards Stacey.

"Look, Stacey. I know the drugs weren't yours. There are hundreds of girls, just like you, who get into trouble in Ibiza because of their boyfriend's drugs. Do you think he would have the same loyalty for you? How do you think we found out about your room and the money? Don't waste your time in prison for someone else's crime. No one will think any less of you. If you help us, we will help you. All we need is names and details then you can walk out of here today, no charge. Are you going to save yourself or him?

"No offence, but this life obviously does not suit you. I can see you're a nice girl. Get out of this whilst you can, start a new life."

Stacey took a deep breath and looked out at the sunshine coming through the tiny office window.

"I'm not going to say anything, till I have someone present."

Diego let out a sigh, shut the folder in front of him, and placed her passport back into a plastic sleeve.

"Very well. It's your choice. I hope you have good, honest, friends, or you could find yourself in big trouble. I will let you know when a representative turns up. Good luck."

"Thank you," Stacey said, praying that she was doing the right thing.

5

"*Pardonna, Señorita* Mears."

A voice brought Stacey back into the room. She'd been dreaming she was locked away in a grubby foreign prison, with no way of getting out. She felt tears come to her eyes as she looked around her cell and at the woman stood in front of her, the realisation that in fact it wasn't a dream starting to sink in.

"I am your representative. My name is Sophia Gonzalez. I need to tell you that you will see the judge in five minutes."

Stacey examined the woman stood over her, she looked so clean and sophisticated, she couldn't understand how she existed on an island like Ibiza.

"Here, take this." Sophia handed Stacey a cup of lukewarm coffee. "I understand you don't want to tell them about your friend's involvement?"

"There is nothing to say. I just need to get out of here, Sophia, and get my stuff back. Do you think they will release me today? I had all my savings in that safe and they weren't from the drugs. If you speak to my employer, Richard from Temptations he will verify what I'm telling you."

"They will not be giving your money back, Stacey, until after the trial, but I will do my best to explain. The judge is going to want to know something. You don't have to tell them why, or how you obtained the drugs, but maybe explain that you are too scared to tell the truth. Maybe they will take pity for you."

Stacey nodded as she drank the coffee, glad that Sophia seemed to be on her side.

"OK, tell them I'm scared but nothing else. I'm not grassing on anyone."

"Very well. The guard will be along shortly to take you to court room. I will be waiting for you inside."

Stacey digested the information, then thanked Sophia for her help. She watched as the door shut behind Sophia, envying her freedom. She still felt severely hung over and couldn't shake the exhaustion that had taken over her body. She downed her coffee, then got off the bed, ready for her judgment.

The room Stacey was led into was more like an office than a court. There were two men and two women, all dressed in suits, sat at a table in the centre of the room who glared at her as she was shown her seat. Stacey knew she must look awful, her hair felt completely matted and on top of that she was finding it hard to see out of her swollen eye.

It wasn't the best way to present herself to the people who were making decisions that could affect the rest of her life. Her hands were so clammy, they made wet imprints on the table as the solemn people in suits took it in turns to speak to Sophia in Spanish.

"They are asking me, how you know the men you were arrested with?"

Stacey felt the eyes of the two women bore into her as she tried to think of her answer.

"They were just some men I met at the bar, opposite my hotel."

Sophia relayed the information to the people around the table. They spoke back to her in Spanish, their voices sounding angry and hurried.

"They are asking if the drugs belonged to you?"

"Yes, they were mine," Stacey replied, briefly allowing herself to meet the scornful faces in front of her.

"And did you intend to distribute this drugs for financial reasons?"

"No, no I didn't."

"And the person you obtained them from, do you have his name? Or location?"

Stacey took a deep breath, remembering what Sophia had advised her to say.

"I'm sorry. I can't say, I'm too scared of what will happen to me, if I do."

There was a lot more heated conversation between the four officials and Sophia, before the room fell deadly quiet.

"A court date has been set in three weeks from now, Stacey. Until then, you cannot leave the island, under *no* circumstances. The judges have set a bail of two thousand euros. If you, or someone else can pay this, you may leave and wait for your sentence. If not, you must go to prison and wait there."

"I had five thousand euros in my room at the Don Juan. The police must have found it. They can use that to pay."

"Unfortunately, as I said, no money found in your room can be used for the bail. It has to be sourced independently."

"What? That's not fair. I don't have any other money!"

"You will have to get it from someone else."

The court officials started to file away the paper in front of them, their faces indignant at the situation taking place.

"You have to listen, Stacey," Sophia said, leaning into her. "That money cannot be used, if you can think of someone who can help you, then we need to sort it out as soon as possible because the court is closing for the day. Come, we must leave here."

Before Stacey had a chance to protest, she was ushered out of the room by one of the guards. Sophia followed behind, her face etched with concern.

"Do you have someone who you can call? Maybe a parent?" Sophia's words cut into Stacey as she realised she had no one. No parents, no friends or boyfriend, she was all alone in the world and the knowledge made her want to break down and cry.

"Can I get my phone?"

"I'm afraid that won't be possible until the morning."

"How can I ring someone, if I can't get to my phone?" she asked, the thought of spending a single second in prison, making her nauseous.

"Property has now closed, so has the court, you were the last hearing. I'm afraid without bail money, they are going to take you to Can Misses Prison. You don't have anyone you could ring now?"

Stacey thought about Lucia, it was the only number she knew off by heart, but she hadn't answered it all those times. *What made her think she would answer it now?* No matter what, it was worth a try, it was not like she had anything to lose.

"I have one."

"OK, you need to come with me so we can ring it now. We only have few minutes; the whole building will be closing soon."

Stacey followed Sophia into a separate smaller office, she could feel the sweat trickle down her back as she dialled the number. Her heart skipped a beat as it started to ring, but after a few seconds it went to voicemail. Stacey put the phone down and redialled, praying she would get an answer. She could feel Sophia's eyes on her as the guard entered the room.

"It's ringing?" she asked, her eyes conveying the hopelessness Stacey was now feeling inside.

Stacey heard the guard speak in Spanish to Sophia, his tone not sounding happy as the phone started to ring again.

"We've got to go now. There is no more calling tonight."

Stacey could hear background noise coming from the speaker in the phone.

"*Bronto?*"

"Lucia! It's me, Stacey." Before she could say any more the phone was put down.

Stacey stared at the receiver in disbelief, tears starting to form in her eyes.

"What happened?" Sophia asked as the guard started to walk towards Stacey.

"She put the phone down on me. I can't believe it!"

"I'm sorry, Stacey, but you have to let the guard take you. I can't help you anymore till tomorrow when everything opens again."

"What? No! I've got numbers on my phone I can ring. I don't want to go to prison."

"Sorry but I have to go now. We will speak tomorrow. Try to get some sleep." Sophia was walked off by one guard as the other wrapped his hands around Stacey's arm.

"This can't be right!" Stacey shouted, pulling away from the guard. "I have people I can call!" Before she could finish her sentence, she felt the strong arms of the guard grab her either side. There was no point protesting any further, she was going to prison.

6

It had been three days since Lucia last slept and the pulse in her head was pounding through her temples, making her wince with every movement. *Why couldn't she find it?*

She was sure she had left it in her suitcase pocket but now it wasn't there. *Had she left it in the room back in Figueretas?*

It was over a month since she had moved in with Salvatore; a month of continual partying and getting high and she hadn't thought to check for her passport, until now.

How could she possibly leave without it? Lucia couldn't believe that she could be so disorganized as to misplace it. Especially now, when she needed to get as far away from this island as possible.

When Lucia had received the message from Nico, asking her to meet him in secret, she'd been dubious. After all, she hadn't seen him since the night at Pacha, when Salvatore had revealed that he was married and had been the whole time they were together. She'd wanted nothing more to do with Nico, and it had come as a relief when Salvatore had forbidden the mention of his former partner's name, claiming him to be a liar and a traitor. Lucia had even convinced herself that she was over Nico and that maybe she could grow to love Salvatore, who obviously cared more about her. Despite her attempts to get over him, when Nico had contacted her, all the old feelings had come rushing back. Try as she might, Lucia couldn't resist the urge to hear him out. So she'd snuck out, past the guards and onto the main road, where Nico was waiting for her. Their meeting had changed everything. Lucia now knew the reasons behind Nico's lies and the knowledge sickened her to her core.

Salvatore was more psychotic than Lucia could ever imagine, and she needed to escape before it was too late but she wouldn't get far without a passport. Not that she had much choice, Nico was waiting for her outside and Salvatore would be expecting her at dinner any minute. She'd taken a risk sneaking out earlier and she was lucky she hadn't been noticed. She emptied her suitcase again, searching its contents for her passport till a noise at the door stopped her in her tracks. She looked up at the source, a chill passed over her body as she saw Salvatore.

"Looking for this?"

Salvatore was standing against the doorframe, her passport in his hands. His eyes were cold and he stared at her with a hardness she'd not seen before.

"You won't be getting very far without it. Where are you going anyway? Finally had enough of partying?"

Lucia's whole body started to shake with fear; trying to hide her emotions she lit a cigarette and kept packing.

"I'm leaving you," she said, as she started to zip up her suitcase.

"You're leaving? Why is that, my love?" Salvatore replied playfully, like a cat toying with a mouse.

"It's my mamma. She is sick. I need to go back to home to see her. I have to be with her. I didn't want to be a burden to you." Lucia could hear the cracks in her voice as she spoke but carried on regardless; aware that her life now depended on what she said next.

"So, you were going to leave me, without saying goodbye?"

"No, of course not. I just knew you'd convince me to stay."

A smile crept across Salvatore's mouth as he flicked her passport in his hands.

"You think highly of yourself, don't you, pussy cat? Do you really think I am such a monster to not let you go to your mamma?"

"No way! You know I care about you. Why would I think you're a monster when you have been nothing but kind to me?"

Salvatore edged forward and placed his finger over her lips.

"Shh, don't worry about these things, my love. I'll make sure to book you a flight first thing tomorrow and I will get Marcellus to accompany you. That way, when your mamma is better, you can come straight back to me. That's if you still want to stay here?"

Salvatore took his finger from Lucia's lips and stood back, his eyes scanning hers.

"Yes, I want nothing more but I need to leave tonight. I can book it myself. I don't need to be accompanied, as I will be coming back, no matter what. So is it possible to get my passport back as I will need it for the flight?" She pushed away the shakes that were threatening to take over her body and stroked Salvatore's arm, indicating the passport in his hand.

"Oh no!" he said, pulling away from her and placing the passport in his pocket. "I couldn't just let you book everything yourself, not with all the stress you have going on.

"It's better if I keep hold of it, I'll need it to book your flight. It's not like you're going to use it till then, is it?"

The tension in the room was unbearable; it was obvious he knew she was planning on running away and he was testing her. If what Nico had told her was true, she would have to be very careful when considering her next move.

"I'm sorry, my love, I didn't want to impose myself on your good nature and I still don't. I'm sure it would be better for you, if I moved out and supported myself from now on."

Lucia could feel the anger pouring out of Salvatore as he turned to her, his eyes wide.

"You want to go? After all I have done?" He grabbed Lucia, digging his fingers into her arms as she yelped out in pain. She could smell a mixture of alcohol and bitter aftershave as he pressed himself against her.

"What are you doing? You know I want to stay! I just don't want to be a burden to you."

The realisation that she was in a bad situation gravitated through Lucia's body as Nico's words echoed through her head. She wondered if he would come to rescue her now, but she seriously doubted it.

"You will stay, and I will book your flight, I might even come with you. It's been a long time since I was in Roma." Salvatore's fingernails were clasping at her flesh, and Lucia could feel his manhood stiffen as his torso pressed against her own. He'd never hurt her before and she was so petrified she daren't fight back.

"OK, I will stay, but please get off me, it's hurting."

Salvatore's eyes searched her own as he loosened his grip on her and grabbed at her face.

"You really are the most exquisite beauty, and you know that I have been very patient.

"You say you want me, but I see no evidence. I won't wait forever."

Salvatore released his grip on her face and walked away from her as Lucia took an involuntary gasp. He had spelt it out to her plain and clear now, she had to show him she wanted him. It was something she had been avoiding ever since she'd moved in with him.

She had been prepared to give herself to him eventually, but how could she contemplate it now?

"That's only if you want me."

Salvatore's words brought Lucia back to the room. *If she didn't play ball with him would he take her by force?* Finding the last of her courage, Lucia composed herself.

"I just wanted it to be perfect with you, yet you become angry like this? Of course I want you. That's why I didn't want to put all this on you. I didn't know about your friend at the airport, otherwise I would have asked you. Obviously I am upset about my mamma, I'm sorry if you feel I've been neglecting you." Lucia came to Salvatore, pressing her head against his chest.

He pulled her mouth towards his, her whole body felt repulsed as he slid his tongue into her, the taste of his cologne was bitter in her mouth, making her pull away.

"What's wrong? I have been patient with you for so long now."

"The time is not right, I am upset about my mamma. Can't we just go for dinner? I'm so hungry."

Salvatore hardened against her, then without warning, he pushed her away causing her to topple onto the floor.

"Salva!" She glanced up at him as he stood against the doorframe, his eyes looking her up and down in disgust.

"You think dinner is enough for me? Believe me, Lucia; I won't be waiting for you for too much longer. As for your mamma, I'm not sure if I can let you go just yet. I will make my decision about it after a couple more days, when things are better between us. Now make yourself presentable, I can't take you out in public like this. You look like a piece of shit. I don't want people to see how much of a junkie you have turned into. Be ready in ten minutes. And Lucia…"

"Yes?" she asked, not daring to get up off the floor.

"Do not fuck with me."

Salvatore didn't wait for an answer and instead walked out of the room. Lucia picked herself off the floor and hurried to get ready. She knew she needed to get away, but she knew that now was not the time.

Ten minutes later and Lucia was escorted by Marcellus to Salvatore's Jaguar. Salvatore didn't even turn to acknowledge her as she got in. It was starting to get dark as the car drove round the back roads of Ibiza. Lucia had to quickly catch her breath as spotted Nico's car, following them from a distance. She smiled inwardly at his audacity, hoping against hope that he had prepared for this outcome.

7

An ear-piercing siren woke Stacey from her deep slumber. Not sure whether she had dreamt it, she rolled over and drifted back off to sleep. Five minutes later, another sounded; this time she bolted up in her bed, hearing movements all around her. She opened her eyes and looked around at her new home; in the light of day she was relieved to see the cell she'd been transported to was pretty decent, compared to the one at the *Policia Nacional Station*. A third siren sounded, and this time the door to her cell was unlocked and opened.

"*Vamos Chica!*" A heavy-set woman dressed in a white shirt and black trousers shouted, jangling her keys in Stacey's direction expectantly. "You have to get up now.

"You do not stay here. Get ready. Five minutes."

The guard gave her a stern look before walking out of the cell. Desperately needing to urinate, Stacey reluctantly pulled herself out of bed and walked towards the toilet in the corner of the room. The early morning chill caused her body to shiver as she squatted over the dirty basin.

Before Stacey even had a chance to pull up her knickers, the guard shouted at her to move from the cell again.

"I can't." Stacey cried out as she stooped by her bed, her feet feeling completely rooted to the spot. Tears started rolling down her crusted eyes as the guard, whose name tag read as Susanna, put her arms round her and, ushered her towards the door. Stacey had never heard such noises coming from her body but she welcomed the relief they brought. Everything that had been building up came flooding out of her as she thought of her mum, Lucia, Aaron, and her lost freedom.

"You must come with me. We will help you all we can."

Stacey examined Susanna through her streaming eyes; she had a look about her that was caring and stern at the same time. The kind of look that told you she would look after you to the best of her capabilities, but if you crossed her you would have hell to pay.

Stacey decided there and then she was going to try to be brave; wiping the tears from her eyes she let Susanna pull her towards the door.

"Thank you *Señorita*. Now we go downstairs."

Stacey's body was still lurched over as she nodded meekly in Susanna's direction.

She followed Susanna's broad shoulders past the other cells, and downstairs to an office. At the desk sat a suited woman with another female guard next to her. There was a girl sitting at the front of the desk, wearing an oversized t-shirt and loose cotton shorts. Her cheeks were blotchy from crying and she had a defeated look on her face. Stacey guessed her to be an inmate and tried to look sympathetically towards her. The woman in the suit glanced at Susanna and then at Stacey. The other inmate gave her a look of recognition, as she was led out of the office by the guard.

"Please be seated," commanded the woman in the suit, in a tone that was both neutral and authoritative. She wasn't the 'usual' Spanish type, with dark skin and eyes Stacey had so far encountered. This woman had fair skin, light brown hair cut into a bob and blue eyes. Stacey felt slightly nervous around her, but at the same time strangely comforted by the look of fairness emanating from her. She pulled out a red file from her cabinet with Stacey's name written on it in black marker.

"I am Rosa, the Senior Manager at Can Misses. Your name is Stacey Mears, is that right?"

Stacey nodded solemnly, wondering if she would need her lawyer present for this conversation.

"I need you to sign these verifications of your ID please." Rosa handed Stacey two sheets of paper with pictures of her passport on them.

Stacey read through them quickly and deciding they were legitimate signed them at the bottom.

"Thank you, Stacey. There is breakfast now. Susanna will take you there."

"Can I make a phone call, please?" Stacey asked Rosa, eager to see if Sophia had managed to retrieve her mobile phone.

"You have a number?"

"No, but she's my representative, she was with me at the court yesterday. I need to speak to her about my bail money."

"OK I see. We can look her up for you and get the details registered by tomorrow."

"Tomorrow? Why tomorrow?" Stacey asked, the panic evident in her voice.

"First you have to register the number, then you have twenty-four hours for it to clear," Rosa replied, her expression unchanging.

"What? That can't be right. I need to get out of here!" Stacey couldn't stop the tears from escaping as she pleaded with Rosa.

"I'm sorry, but it's the rules. You register the number, then you call the next day."

Before Stacey could protest any further, Susanna placed her arms around her and beckoned her to the canteen. There were twelve girls sat around a table eating breakfast out of plastic trays. Their eyes widened as Stacey was led to a seat on a separate, smaller table. No matter how hard she tried, she couldn't compose herself. With her head ducked down she continued to sob, not caring about the food placed in front of her or the looks she was receiving from the other inmates. Stacey watched as her tears dripped onto the table. Thoughts of her mother entered her head; *How many times had she visited her inside and swore to herself that it would never be her?* The irony of the situation was not lost on her. She'd come to Ibiza to escape her mother's lifestyle and instead found herself in just as much trouble.

Stacey watched through the window of the canteen as the other inmates headed to the outside courtyard, noting how they seemed divided into two groups. The larger of the groups positioned themselves around the tables in the shade. Their make-up-less faces seemed miserable, but harmless enough as they lit up cigarettes and started to play cards.

The smaller group, who had already started to get undressed, placed themselves on mats in the open part of the yard, directly under the sun's rays. Two of the girls, both blonde with a hint of make-up on their faces, stuck out to Stacey. They looked so glamorous and carefree as they sunbathed in their bikinis. Stacey couldn't understand how they managed to keep it together. She felt horrendous; glancing down at her legs, she could see her mosquito bites had formed into unsightly scabs and in between her toes there was a brown residue were dirt had now formed. She grimaced to herself as she examined the now stained and dusty black dress she'd been wearing since she was arrested.

"Rosa want to see you. Come," Susanna told her, smiling softly at Stacey.

She followed Susanna to the office where she was greeted by Rosa's neutral face.

We have some clothes here for you, if you want to choose, and a towel. If you want to shower, Susanna will take you afterwards." Rosa indicated a cardboard box on the floor.

It was as if they had read Stacey's mind, rummaging through the box she was reminded of a summer in her childhood spent in a hostel. Her mum had been forced into hiding after one of her psycho ex-boyfriends had threatened to kill her. Like most of the women they'd had to abandon all their possessions. A charity founded for women in crisis would bring boxes of toys and clothes for them weekly and it would be the highlight of the hostel, even though most of the time there would be fights over the 'best stuff'. This time Stacey was able to pick in peace and she selected some blue shorts and a t-shirt with a Spanish slogan on it that she didn't understand. She put the clothes to her nose and inhaled, they smelt clean and she was relieved. Susanna escorted her to the shower as she started crying again, this time not because she was sad but because for the first time in a long time, she actually felt safe.

8

Lucia was greeted with smiles and kisses as she entered Salvatore's restaurant, *Il Dalia Nero.* The restaurant was so authentically Italian, it never failed to transport Lucia back home, and for that reason she normally loved coming there. Tonight was different, Salvatore had invited Marcellus, his Albanian security guard, to join them for dinner. It was obvious that he wanted to keep an eye on her, and she knew that if she tried to challenge him it would end very badly. So she smiled back and sat down at the table like there was nothing wrong, waiting for her first opportunity to escape.

"So, *amore,* what are you having to eat? Or do you just prefer that I give you your dessert as per usual?" Salvatore addressed her with danger in his eyes and Lucia chose her next words carefully.

"Thank you, Salva, but I will eat first tonight. The carbonara always looks good when you have it, so I will try that."

"The carbonara? This is not your usual salad. Will you be eating it? Or just moving it around on your plate like normal?" Even though it was said in jest, there was no warmth in Salvatore's eyes as he spoke her.

"No, no. Tonight I am hungry and I promise this time I will eat it all." Lucia couldn't remember the last time she had consumed a proper meal. Before her meeting with Nico, each day had seemed to fade into the next, as she attended party after party, sometimes staying awake for up to four days at a time. Her meeting with Nico had invoked an epiphany within Lucia; no longer did she want to be numb to her life. She hadn't touched any drugs for nearly twelve hours and as the chemicals started to leave her system she found a new clarity of thought, as well as an uncontrollable hunger.

"OK then, I will order for you but you better eat it all. You know I don't like waste.

"Now what are you having to drink? Will it be water, to go with your new healthy lifestyle?"

"No, I'll have a wine please. Chardonnay."

"Oh, so you haven't completely changed! Well let's get a bottle in for the princess and remember what I said, don't waste a single drop or no dessert."

"It won't be a problem," Lucia said, her body feeling like it could drop with exhaustion at any minute. Salvatore's phone rang and to Lucia's relief he excused himself, leaving Marcellus and herself at the table. The wine showed up and Lucia started to drink it rapidly. She started to notice the disapproving looks from the other

245

people at the tables around her, and realised she was swaying. Without cocaine or food to counteract the glass of wine she had just drunk, she was instantly intoxicated. Salvatore reappeared, his face clouded over like he was ready to kill. Lucia shuddered as Nico's warning rang through her head. *How had she not seen for herself how much of a psycho he was?*

The food was brought to the table, breaking the tension in the air. Lucia ate her steaming plate of carbonara, relishing every mouthful. She felt like her whole body had come alive and she instantly managed to regain some of her composure. She tried to finish the whole plate, but her stomach had shrunk so much she ended up having to leave over half of it. Not that Salvatore seemed to notice, the blood dribbling down the side of his mouth as he tore into his steak.

Nico had always warned her that Salvatore was a dangerous man, yet after the night at Amnesia, Lucia had thought she'd seen a different side to him. Now, she realised that it had all been an act; an act that she'd been completely oblivious to. She'd thought nothing of being escorted everywhere by Marcellus, or the random checks he had carried out on her phone. In her moments of drug-fuelled lunacy, she'd even gone so far as to tell Salvatore she cared about him. Now all Lucia wanted to do was to run away as far as possible, but it was clear that Salvatore wouldn't give her up without a fight. Not that Lucia would let that get in her way of escaping. If she had to go without her passport, then that was what she would do, she couldn't stand to be around him a moment longer. Once she escaped Lucia would find Stacey, and try to make amends for what had happened.

Stacey had been a victim of addiction all her life, and Lucia felt ashamed of what she had put her through. If she could just speak face-to-face with Stacey, maybe she could make her understand *why* she acted the way she did.

"Ah, so you *were* hungry tonight. Good. Maybe you won't look so much like a walking corpse. I swear you're starting to scare me with this face. Anyway, as promised, I have your dessert."

Salvatore handed Lucia a wrap which she quickly placed in her handbag. Excusing herself from the table, she headed to the toilets. Marcellus looked up from his phone, his eyes meeting hers with what she could have sworn was a warning glance. She locked herself in a cubicle and pulled out the wrap of cocaine, tipping a little down the toilet, just to be safe. She checked her phone for the first time since she'd left the villa; her heart almost stopped when she saw a text from Nico.

"I am always watching you bambina and am waiting patiently for the chance to rescue you. Please tell me you are OK?"

Lucia wrote back, her hands sweating over the keys.

"I tried to escape but he had my passport and caught me before I could leave. I am at the Dahlia with him but afterwards I will escape without my passport." To Lucia's relief, Nico texted back within seconds.

"I will wait for you tonight in the usual spot. Any trouble call me and I will come.

Be careful Lucia."

Lucia deleted the messages and came out of the toilet, catching a glimpse of herself in the mirror. Salvatore was right; her skin was dull from the days she'd spent in her bed with a comedown and her cheek bones, poking out of her gaunt face, made her look like a corpse. It was the look she remembered sporting after she'd run away from home. She'd fallen for a drug dealer called Christian, who took more cocaine than he sold. Lucia had soon found herself also hooked on the drug, spending vast amounts of her savings getting them high, and bailing him out. When some well-connected Sicilians turned up at their door looking for retribution, Lucia had ended up with a gun in her sobbing face, as they beat Christian unconscious. It didn't deter her from her destructive lifestyle, she just got even higher so she could forget it all. Finding Christian in bed with another woman had probably saved her life. She finally saw their relationship for what it was, and she used the last of her savings to book herself a one way ticket to London, vowing to never get in that way again.

A loud knocking came from outside the door, bringing Lucia out of her thoughts. She patted water on her face, took a deep breath, and headed outside.

"You took your time. What were you doing in there?" Marcellus asked, snarling at her as she walked towards him.

Lucia ignored him and carried on walking to the table. She took her seat next to Salvatore and reached for her wine.

"So, did you like your dessert?" Salvatore's voice was animated as he spoke to her.

"Yes thank you, my generous love."

"What's that noise?" Salvatore asked, indicating to the vibrating sound coming from her bag.

"What noise?" Lucia replied, a wave of fear rushing over her as she realised it was coming from her phone.

"That vibrating. It's coming from your bag. It must be your phone."

"No, I don't think so, are you sure?" To Lucia's relief, her phone stopped vibrating.

"Get your phone out. I want to check who it is."

"It was nothing, I probably just pressed on some keys by mistake."

"Marcellus get her phone."

Marcellus forced his way into Lucia's bag and grabbed her phone. She watched helplessly as it started to vibrate again in his huge hand.

"It's ringing."

"Yes I can hear that. What does the number say?"

"It's a local number, I don't recognize it."

"Well pass it to Lucia then, I'm sure she will want to know who it is, won't you?"

Marcellus passed it to Lucia, who clasped it in her shaking hands.

"Answer it, now!" Salvatore shouted at her, his eyes wild.

Lucia reluctantly pressed the answer button and slowly took the phone to her ear, praying it wasn't Nico.

"Bronto?"

"Lucia! It's me, Stacey." Instantly, Lucia put the phone down.

"What the fuck are you playing at Lucia? Who was it?" Salvatore asked, spitting his words into Lucia's face.

"I don't know, baby. I think it was wrong number." Lucia couldn't believe Stacey had just tried to call her. She felt awful for putting the phone down on her but her first instinct was to protect her from Salvatore. No way was she going to let him get his hands on Stacey, like he had done with her. She remembered how Salvatore had constantly grilled her on Stacey's whereabouts and their relationship together. She'd assumed it was out of concern for their friendship, but knowing what she did about Salvatore now, she knew his intentions were far from innocent. He wanted them both with him and luckily, so far she'd been able to convince him that Stacey and she would never be reunited. If Salvatore found out otherwise, who knew what he would be capable of?

"Wrong number? Do you think I'm some sort of idiot?"

"No of course not," Lucia said, trying to smile as she put her phone back in her bag.

"Give me the phone."

"Honest to God, it was a wrong…"

"Give me the phone now!" Salvatore shouted, making the whole restaurant fall into a stunned silence.

"I am going to find out who has called you Lucia, and God help you if you're lying."

Lucia nodded, the fear in her rising as she watched Salvatore pocket her phone, silently praying to herself that Stacey would not be calling her back.

Trapped

1

It was Stacey's third day in Can Misses Prison and for the first time in a long time, she woke up feeling relatively stress-free. Yesterday she'd spoken to her solicitor, Sophia, who'd explained that there'd been a new development in her case. The Newcastle lads she'd been arrested with had been summoned to court. During questioning, they'd admitted that the drugs seized belonged to the whole group, and that Stacey had only been holding them.

Stacey had not been expecting them to be so honest; part of her had thought that they would leave her to rot in prison. Their confessions meant that the charge of distribution would be dropped and the amount of drugs she'd been caught with would be divided between the group. Still, without the money to secure her bail, she would have to wait in prison till her court date, three weeks away. Stacey didn't mind too much, her mother had always harped on about how life was a lot simpler inside, and at this moment in time she had to agree with her. There was no worrying about gangsters, druggie best friends, providing a roof over her head, securing three meals a day, or dealing with men who just wanted to use her. She had full access to the prison's recreational centre and a yard outside where she could laze about sunbathing all day; it was almost like being on holiday. It's not like she had a lot waiting for her outside, she'd tried to make contact with Lucia but it was obvious she wanted nothing more to do with her, much like Aaron, who'd blanked her since she'd confessed all to him. Even if she did get released, she would probably have to dance again just to afford to go back home, the place she had run away from. She wasn't even sure she could dance anymore, all the strength she'd once possessed had whittled away and she now felt like an empty shell of a person. She hadn't bothered to register any numbers for today, there was no one she wanted to speak to. She preferred to wait inside until her trial and if that made her a quitter, then so be it, she was fed up with trying.

Stacey followed the other inmates as they made their way to the canteen for breakfast.

She scanned the room for somewhere to sit and noticed her new cell mate, Maria, calling her over. With her deeply wrinkled face that echoed what must have been a hard life, and numerous gold chains, she wasn't someone Stacey would usually want to bunk with. At first, she had thought it better to keep herself to herself, but Maria had other ideas. She'd tried her hardest to converse with Stacey in broken bits of English, mixed with Spanish and some crazy hand gestures. Despite her initial misconceptions, as Maria forced biscuits and an extra blanket on her, Stacey started to warm towards the idea that they could be friends. It was obvious Maria was well liked in the prison, and it soon became apparent that Stacey had been put with her because of this reason, and for that she was grateful.

Stacey took the seat next to Maria, who was conversing loudly in Spanish with some of the inmates, all of whom were hysterical with laughter. For a brief moment, Stacey wondered if they were talking about her, but when she heard the warmth in Maria's husky voice and saw the big gappy smile she gave her when she sat down, she knew she was just being paranoid. She took a deep, contented breath, and tucked into her delicious omelette.

Life wasn't so bad here, and if she had to stay a bit longer then it wouldn't be the end of the world.

"Stacey. I need you to come to the office."

All the inmates looked up as Susanna stood in front of them. Stacey felt her cheeks redden as she followed her to the office.

"Come inside. Thank you, Susanna." Stacey felt relieved when Rosa smiled at her as she entered the room. Susanna nodded, giving Stacey a knowing look as she shut the door.

"I have some good news for you." Rosa shuffled her paper work as she spoke. "You are to be released this afternoon."

"What? How?"

"You seem upset with the news?"

"No. No. Just a bit shocked, that's all."

"Your friend has paid the money for your release, so as soon as we sort out the paper work you will be free from here."

"Friend? What friend?"

"It doesn't say here but they obviously knew about you being detained."

"I can't believe it. I don't have any friends who know I'm here."

"Well that's not possible, otherwise how would they know to pay for you? Anyway get your stuff ready and we will prepare for your release in the next few hours."

"Few hours! Is there any way you can find out who paid my bail?"

"I can try for you but surely it does not matter, if you are free?"

"Yeah I suppose so." Stacey was in utter disbelief as she walked out of the office. *Who could have released her?* The only person she had rung was Lucia and they didn't even talk. Part of her hoped it was her but there was this niggling feeling that maybe something wasn't right about this situation. Either way, in less than three hours she would find out and once again be a free woman. Stacey tried to make herself happy about it, but try as she might, she couldn't shake off the impending sense of dread that had started to loom over her.

2

The bright afternoon sun obstructed Stacey's view as she looked out for her mysterious benefactor waiting behind the gates of Can Misses Prison. Shielding her eyes, she nearly ran back inside when she spotted an unknown black car with what looked like two men in the driver and passenger seat. A woman wearing a pair of oversized sunglasses emerged from the back. Despite being uncharacteristically wobbly on her feet and having lost a lot of weight there was no denying it was Lucia. From a distance, Lucia's long black hair and glasses hid her expression and Stacey walked towards her hesitantly. When she got closer and saw the familiar warm smile plastered across Lucia's face, she couldn't help but run to her. She nearly burst into tears when she felt Lucia's arms around her body. She smelt like alcohol and way too many parties but Stacey didn't care, she'd missed her friend so much, all her previous trepidation over them ever been able to reunite completely disappeared.

"It's so good to see you, my baby," Lucia said, her voice choking up as she took off her glasses,

"It's so good to see you too. Thank you so much for bailing me out. Are you OK? Who are you with?"

Up close, Stacey was shocked to see how bad Lucia actually looked. Her usually glowing olive skin had a dull yellowy tinge to it and her emerald green eyes were watery and blood shot. Before Lucia had a chance to answer, the passenger door to the car opened and a man in a black suit got out..

He walked towards them, his dark hair slicked back into a ponytail, the majority of his face was hidden by huge black sunglasses but Stacey instantly recognized him as the man from Amnesia, Salvatore. Aaron's warning came flashing into her thoughts but she pushed it out After all, Salvatore had come to rescue her, *what had Aaron done?*

"*Buono serra,* Stacey. It is my pleasure to finally meet you." The smell of Salvatore's peppery aftershave was so overpowering Stacey started to cough as he leant in to kiss both her cheeks

"Thank you so much for rescuing me from there." Stacey replied, managing to regain her composure. "I promise I will get the money back to both of you as soon as I can."

Salvatore smiled at Stacey and then looked over at Lucia who had her glasses back on, her gaze concentrated on the ground.

"Please don't worry about the money. Lucia cares very much for you, and a friend of Lucia's is, of course, a friend of mine. Is there anywhere we can take you? If not, you are more than welcome to rest at my home until you decide on something else."

"Well, I've been kicked me out of my hotel and the Guardia have taken my money so I'm kind of stranded. If it's OK, I could really do with having some rest at your place and catching up with Lucia?"

Stacey noticed Lucia's bottom lip droop in response, like she wasn't happy at the thought of her staying. Stacey dismissed the idea instantly, *of course Lucia wanted her to stay, otherwise why would she have come to rescue her in the first place?*

The solemn faced driver put her bag in the boot of the car as Stacey followed Lucia to the back seat. She had to stop herself screaming out in pain as Lucia dug her nails into her arm and leant into Stacey's ear, her voice so quiet, she had to strain in order to hear her.

"You must do as I say baby. You must trust me. Salvatore is dangerous but I have a plan. I tell you everything later, OK? For now just play along. *Ti amo* Stacey. I am so sorry for this, really. I missed you so much *amore*. I would never put you in this trouble on purpose."

It dawned on Stacey that this wasn't the simple rescue mission it had first appeared.

Lucia wasn't with Salvatore of her own accord, she was in danger and now thanks to her incarceration, so was Stacey.

"Let's just go. Take my hand, we can run towards the prison and get them to take us in.

"We don't need any more trouble."

"Baby, he won't think twice to shoot us." Tears rolled down Lucia's face as the car door opened and Salvatore got into the front. He removed his glasses and turned to face them, his huge, jade green eyes examining them as his thin lips formed into a smile.

"You both look like you've accepted a ride with the devil!" he laughed, as Lucia quickly wiped the tears from her face. "Has Lucia explained everything to you?" Stacey nodded, her eyes staring directly into his.

"Good. Now let's go. I hope Lucia has mentioned that you don't fuck with me, or you don't have a very nice life, *Capiche*?"

"Yes, I understand," Stacey replied, her voice tainted with anger as she watched the prison gates fade into the background.

The sky was becoming darker and the shadows from the trees were starting to form on the ground as Salvatore's driver navigated them through the forested back roads of Ibiza.

"Where are we going?" Lucia asked in English, her hand still in Stacey's. "This is not the way to your house?"

Salvatore started laughing, a chilling laugh, that made the small hairs on Stacey's arms stand to attention.

"So perceptive, Lucia. This is what the Francese call a *detour*. All will be revealed to you soon, so try to relax. We have a long night ahead of us."

Lucia looked terrified at his response and squeezed Stacey's hand harder in her own. Stacey took deep breaths trying to expel the mounting tension rising within her. She spotted the brightly-lit bungee rope that marked the entrance to San Antonio in the distance and hoped that whether they were being taken it wouldn't be their final destination.

3

"What is this place?" Lucia asked as they pulled into a car park behind a boarded up building with a sign on the roof spelling out the word *Extasis*, in unlit bulbs.

"My Lucia, do not worry about where we are, or why. All you need to worry about is doing what I say. *Capiche?*"

Both Stacey and Lucia nodded as he turned to them, the look in his eyes daring them to challenge him.

"Both of you get out and follow me inside." He spoke to the driver in Italian as Lucia face dropped behind her glasses.

"What are you doing? Keep walking!" The driver hissed as Stacey crouched down on the gravelly car park outside the car.

"I feel sick," Stacey said clutching onto her stomach with one hand, and grabbing the biggest rock she could off the floor with the other.

"Keep moving," The driver grunted behind her, forcibly taking her arm and leading her to the back entrance of the building. He pushed her towards a dimly lit bar were Lucia and Salvatore were waiting as six men started to emerge from the darkness in front of them. The shadows on their faces made them look like they were wearing grotesque masks and Stacey could see they were all wearing guns around their hips. She forced herself not to react; if Lucia and she were ever going to get out of this situation, she could not let herself be overcome with the terror that was rising within her. Salvatore spoke to the men in Italian and the inside lights were switched on, illuminating the dome shaped interior of the club.

Stacey quickly stashed the rock into her elasticated knickers, courtesy of Can Misses prison, and pulled her baggy t-shirt over the top. She tried to examine the layout, looking for any signs of an exit which would enable their escape. There were three caverns located at the back of the room with two neon fire-exit signs nestled between them. If a miracle happened and they managed to get away, those doors would definitely be where she'd head to first.

"Welcome to Extasis! Ladies, please be seated." Salvatore indicated to the stools facing the bar.

Stacey linked her hand with Lucia's and stood firm. Salvatore narrowed his eyes and a smile started to creep across his face.

"Marcellus. Make these ladies sit." He spoke in English, his huge eyes staring directly at Stacey.

Marcellus marched towards Stacey, ripping her hand away from Lucia's. He pulled her arm behind her back as another man did the same to Lucia. Unable to resist his grip on her arm, Stacey was pushed onto a stool at the opposite side of the bar to Lucia.

"See, it's not so bad, doing what I say, eh? *Allora,* let me make you a drink." Both Stacey and Lucia remained silent as Salvatore walked behind the bar. He rummaged through the glass bottles on the shelf as Stacey willed herself not to look back at Marcellus and the men behind.

"Whisky OK for you? Or maybe you want some cocaine, like your friend? Either way, I won't take no for an answer. Lucia will have a drink and some cocaine. Won't you, *amore?*"

Salvatore spoke to Lucia like she was a child, yet there was an undeniable threat in his voice.

"*No grazie*, Salva. I just want that we go home. I don't understand why we are here."

"Have you heard this? She wants to know why she is here!" His eyes widened as he placed the two drinks in front of Lucia and Stacey. "To our health!" He shouted, his voice echoing across the room as raised his glass in the air. Neither of the girls raised their glasses to meet him.

"I said, to our health!" Salvatore hissed at them, causing the brown liquid inside the glass to spill over, as he slammed his drink onto the bar.

Stacey lifted her glass hesitantly in the air and glanced over at Lucia, whose expression was like that of a terrified animal who was about to be slaughtered.

"Good! Now drink!" Salvatore's eyes bored into Stacey as she took the glass to her mouth, the smell of the whisky turning her stomach. She didn't want to drink it, but the danger in Salvatore's eyes left her with little choice. She sipped on the brown liquid, wincing as she did so. Salvatore downed his in one, then reaching inside his pocket he produced a plastic baggie of cocaine which he emptied onto the bar. He used a bar mat to scrape the cocaine into three massive lines, and sniffing a giant one to himself, he handed Lucia a rolled note.

"For you, *amore mio*."

Lucia's face was pressed into a frown as she pushed the note away.

"I don't want it."

"What? You are telling me that you, the fucking junkie, don't want some cocaine?

"Do not try to be good in front of your friend, we all know what you are, so stop trying to make me angry and take it."

"No." Lucia sat up and stared at Salvatore, the fire almost returning to her eyes. "I won't do it."

Salvatore smiled at her, then slowly he reached inside his jacket pocket. He pulled out a silver handgun, which he pointed at Lucia.

"Take it. I won't ask you again."

Lucia's hand trembled as she took the note and reached towards the line. It was so big she found it hard to finish, which seemed to infuriate Salvatore even more. He pressed the gun against her head, making her sob as she tried to inhale the pile of powder before her.

Stacey reached inside her knickers for the rock, encasing it within her fist. Salvatore was leant over the bar and she knew if she stretched, she would be able to strike him over the head with it.

"Finish it!"

"Salvatore, stop it. It's obvious she can't do it."

"Oh, the fucking English *putta* has a voice." He turned his attention, and his gun, towards Stacey as Lucia finished her line.

"Good. Now your turn." He took the note from Lucia's hand and chucked it towards Stacey. She carefully moved her hand out of her knickers and picked up the note, inhaling the line, to her surprise, in one go. Instantly, the adrenalin surged to her brain and she coughed as the impact of the bitter powder hit the back of her throat.

"So you are a junkie! Just like your friend. Perfect! Two junkie *puttas*!" He spoke in Italian to the men located around the room as Lucia's face turned pale. She turned to Stacey and tried to mouth some words at her, but she couldn't understand what Lucia was trying to say. Two of the men disappeared into the right hand corner of the room, returning with a hunched over man. Stacey could just about see that his face had been cut several times, and that his right eye was swollen and almost black with bruising. He was wearing a blood-stained bandanna and the recognition swarmed into her thoughts. It was Tomas, the guy they had been searching for ever since they had discovered the drugs. His hands were tied behind his back, and he was stumbling as the henchmen paraded him in front of the bar.

The cocaine was causing Stacey's heart to beat really fast and she felt sick but she willed herself to look impartial as Tomas was sat down on a chair in front of her.

"No hello for your friends? That's not nice, especially when they have been looking for you for such a long time." Salvatore spoke to his men in Italian, and they removed the gag from around Tomas' mouth.

"Now tell me Tomas, how do you know these ladies?"

Tomas remained silent, his face despondent. Salvatore spoke again to his guards in Italian and within seconds one stepped forward and punched Tomas in his already bruised eye socket. It immediately started to bleed and Tomas spluttered blood as he cried out in pain. Stacey could tell he was a broken man, he was almost unrecognizable from the carefree guy Lucia and she had met in Space.

"Now Tomas, answer my fucking question."

Tomas looked to the ground as he responded, his voice devoid of any strength.

"They are the girls who took the drugs."

The atmosphere suddenly went from tense to unbearable, and Stacey reached inside her knickers, clenching her hand tighter around the rock inside.

"How did they take the drugs, Tomas?"

"I told you, they must have been put in the English one's bag. I know nothing about it all.

"I was just doing my job."

"This is not true Salva! You know me, you know I take nothing from no one, the same for my friend." Lucia had obviously gained some strength from the coke she'd taken as she pleaded with Salvatore but. Stacey could see her effort was futile; Salvatore was omitting a dark energy that couldn't be relinquished.

He walked towards Lucia as Stacey geared herself up, ready to strike him if she needed to. She held her breath as he reached past them both, scooping up the left over cocaine from the bar with his fingers and delivering it into his large nostrils. With the white powder over his face, he picked a glass up from the shelf and inspected it like a vase in a shop, his eyes swimming wildly in their sockets. He threw the glass onto the stone floor making Lucia and Stacey cry out, as the shards shattered around their feet.

"You going to fucking lie to me?" His eyes changed from wide to enormous and he lunged at Lucia, grabbing her by the throat.

"Get off her!" Stacey cried out as Marcellus secured her arms.

Salvatore released his grip on Lucia, sending her crashing to the ground.

"Let us start again. Tomas, would you be so kind to tell us who you saw the girls with the day they stole the drugs?"

"They were with Aaron Conroy," Tomas said, so quietly it was almost inaudible.

Marcellus re-gagged Tomas as Lucia's eyes darted across to Stacey's.

Lucia who was still on the ground, looked shocked by the revelation, yet she quickly diverted her attention back towards Salvatore.

"We don't know anything about this Aaron, Salva. She has said the truth, now please, let us go."

"Alfonso, please show to the lying putta that we are serious."

Alfonso grabbed Lucia off the floor by the throat and dangled her mid-air. Stacey tried to move towards her but it was too late. With an effortless force, Marcellus punched her in the head, and she fell onto the floor. Disorientated and in pain, Stacey had no choice but to watch helplessly from the ground as Lucia was dragged, kicking and screaming, to the centre of the room. Stacey tried to pull herself up, but a searing pain shot through her body as Salvatore's crocodile-skin shoe crunched into her hand. She attempted to look over at Lucia, but Salvatore was now shadowing her, his face twisted into a mocking smile.

"So, what were you saying about our friend, Mr. Conroy?" he asked, digging his heel further into Stacey's hand till it felt like it was going to break.

"We didn't give him the drugs." She could hear Lucia gurgling in the background. "Please stop this. You're going to kill her!" Stacey was crying as she slowly reached inside her knickers for the rock. Using all her strength she crashed it onto Salvatore's foot causing him to cry out in pain. Pushing herself up, she headed over to Lucia. But before she could even reach her, she was tackled to the ground by Marcellus as Salvatore leant over her.

"You stupid fucking English *putta*!" He spat in her face as he spoke to her. "You really have pissed me off. I was willing to accept that you were both innocent victims but not now. Federico, get me her mobile!"

He grabbed Stacey and forced her head in the direction of Lucia who was suspended in the air, her face starting to lose its colour as she struggled to get free.

"If it isn't Romeo himself!" Salvatore said, Stacey's mobile in his hands. "And they say romance is dead. Yet here he is asking where you have disappeared to!" Salvatore pressed his gun against Stacey's head.

"My patience is running out." Using his other hand, he pressed the call button on Stacey's phone and passed it to her. "Tell him you want that he meets you here in Extasis. Make it believable and I let your putta friend live. If you don't, you all will die. No pressure."

Stacey's hands trembled as she took the phone into her hand, her heart sank when she heard it start to ring.

"Stacey? I've been trying to call you. Are you OK?"

"Yes, yes I'm fine. Listen, I need you to meet me."

"What's going on? You don't sound too good." Her eyes widened at his correct diagnosis of the situation, but with Salvatore watching her she quickly pulled herself together.

"I've definitely been better, but look I need your help. Can you come and get me please?"

"What's happened? Are you OK?"

Stacey hated that he sounded so sincere and that she could be sentencing him to death but she knew Lucia didn't have much longer to wait.

"Everything is fine. I just need you to come and get me. I'm in this club called Extasis, it's in San Antonio."

"Fucking hell, Stace. What you doing there?"

"I will explain everything when you get here. Just promise me you will come alone. Oh and bring my hat. I'm going to need it." There was a long silence and Stacey willed him to answer.

271

"Hat? OK. I'll be there. See you soon."

"OK. Thank you so much." Stacey ended the call and rushed over to Lucia who was lying lifeless on the floor. "You fucking cunts! What have you done to her?" Stacey took Lucia into her arms and rocked her side to side. Her eyes were shut but as she heard her gasp for air she let out a cry of relief. She wasn't dead but then again, maybe soon they'd both wish they were.

4

The whole room fell silent as a car was heard skidding into the car park behind. Still cradling Lucia in her arms, Stacey watched in horror as Salvatore's henchmen quickly positioned themselves around the room, ready for their upcoming ambush.

"Stacey! It's me, are you in there? Let me in." Aaron called, his fists pounding on the fire exit door.

The door was opened and before Aaron had a chance to run, he was dragged inside. Instantly, he held his hands in the air, allowing the men to search his body at gun point. A black gun was discovered from inside his pocket and with his hands now behind his back, he was marched into the centre of the room.

"*Signore* Conroy, so good of you to come and meet us at such short notice."

Aaron's expression changed from calm to shocked as he noticed Lucia's bloodied face.

"Stacey, are you OK? What have they done to Lucia?"

"They were going to kill her. I'm sorry, I had no choice." she explained holding back her tears.

"What did I tell you earlier about shutting your mouth?" Salvatore snarled, pointing his gun in Stacey's direction.

"It's OK, babe, you don't have to say anymore. I don't know what twisted plan these scum bags are trying to pull off but I can assure you, that you *will* be getting out of here and that if they ever come anywhere near you again, I'll make sure their death is so slow and painful they'll be begging to be finished off. As for you," he turned to the men holding him at gunpoint, then to Salvatore, his face curled up in disgust, "my family has a pact with you, you can't just go kidnapping these girls and torturing them. I would advise you to let them and me go, before you wind up doing something you can't take back."

Salvatore's eyes met Aaron's and a smile started to spread across his face.

"You think I am scared of your *family*?"

"If you're not, then you're signing your own death warrant. Now do as say and let these girls go."

"The girls are going nowhere, brother, and neither are you."

Stacey turned around to face the voice that was coming from the darkness.

"What the fuck are you doing here?" Aaron asked his eyes on the gun now placed in between his eyes.

"Aw! It's my big brother, come to save the day!"

"Do you want to explain to me why you've got a fucking gun pointed at my head Jim?"

Stacey felt her heartbeat pound out of her chest as she watched the scene before her unfold. Lucia was trying her best to sit up; her neck was still badly wounded and the whites of her eyes were showing as she strained to see what was going on.

"Don't pretend you don't know.

"What's the matter? Couldn't bear to see me make something of myself?"

From where she was lying on the ground, Stacey could just make out a couple of faint track marks on Jimmy's arms. His hand was shaking as he pointed the gun at Aaron and the look in his eyes was more desperate than serious. It was obvious to Stacey that he wasn't as assured about the situation as he was making out.

"Jimmy, please believe me, Aaron has nothing to do with this! He never took the drugs and neither did we. I swear to you, this is some sort of set up!"

"Shut the fucking *putta* up now, Marcellus!"

Marcellus bounded towards Stacey and she could feel the cold metal of his gun against her temple.

"OK, OK," Stacey called out, as Lucia clung to her.

"So you've picked a gobby one this time, bro. What happened to Fabs? Did you get fed up of her, when she wasn't yours to steal anymore?"

"The girl who ended up in a wheel chair because of your mate here. I see he's done a good job of brainwashing you."

"Brainwashed? You want to shut your fucking mouth. You think I can't run an operation on my own? You don't know anything about me."

"You are aware that he will screw you over at the first opportunity aren't you, Jimbo?"

"Shut your fucking spoilt mouth. You think just because you're the golden boy that everyone has got to do what you say? Sending me to rehab, whilst you and my Fabs cozied up together. Then when I come out of that shithole by total fucking coincidence, Fabs dumps me, told me it was for the best, the fucking slag, but I knew it was you. You didn't like me having something better than you, did you? You have to have everyone at your command. Now look at you, not such the big man, are ya?"

"Come on, you can't be serious?" Aaron stood up and put his hand over Jimmy's gun as the four surrounding men clicked their weapons in response.

"OK, OK, I'll take it you're serious," Aaron said, sitting back down.

"Deadly," Jimmy said, spitting on the ground.

Stacey couldn't help but be fascinated by the similarities between Aaron and Jimmy now they were next to each other. Both of them had the same square jaw that on Aaron made him look brooding but on Jimmy made his face slightly too angular, emphasizing how undernourished he was. The deep brown eyes that she loved on Aaron's face were a stark comparison to Jimmy's sunken, lighter ones. Everything about him screamed addict, which made it even more suspicious that a man like Salvatore would be the one supporting him.

"Shoot me if it'll make you feel better, Jim, but rest assured, he will kill you next. You think he gives a shit about you?"

The look in Jimmy's eyes showed that he registered Aaron's words but his face remained expressionless.

"You gonna listen to this fake gangster, Jimmy? Fucking shoot him. He take your career, he take your woman, he don't give a shit about you."

Stacey could see by the way Salvatore was clenching his jaw that he was starting to get agitated yet Jimmy didn't even acknowledge him. Instead, he was staring directly at Aaron.

"Was it you that robbed my apartment, Jimmy? You know that Fabianna was targeted there. I was the one who had to tell her mum why she had been shot in the leg. I know you wouldn't have wanted her to be hurt, no matter what you thought had gone on. Did he order the robbery? Do you really fucking trust him?"

Salvatore came towards Aaron and pressed his gun into his temple. Aaron didn't react, his face wholly concentrated on Jimmy's. A moment of hesitation passed on Jimmy's face, before he straightened himself up.

"You knew I loved her, but that wasn't enough for you, was it? Now you have this new girl, like Fabs was nothing."

His comment was directed at Stacey and she couldn't help but feel annoyed that she was now being compared to a woman she'd never even met.

"There is nothing between us Jim, and there never was. I wouldn't do that to you."

The sweat trickled down the side of Salvatore's forehead as he pressed his gun further into Aaron.

"If you don't shoot him, Jimmy, then I will. This man take everything from you. You heard Tomas, it was him who ordered the *puttas* to take your drugs. Now shoot this traitor who's made your life hell. Get it over with. Like we discussed, like you wanted."

"He's fucking with you, Jim. Can't you see that he has instrumented this whole situation to take us down?"

"Shoot him, Jimmy!"

Salvatore's hand started to press down on the trigger and Stacey knew that if she didn't intervene now there would be no more Aaron. Lucia was still huddled against her and out of the corner of her eye, Stacey spotted her sliding her mobile into her pocket. It was obvious she'd just been using it but Stacey had no time to think about it as a plan formed in her mind.

"Move with me towards the rock and on the count of three get out of the way," she hissed in Lucia's ear.

Lucia shuffled her body with Stacey, allowing her to grab the rock. Within seconds, Stacey jumped up and slammed the rock into Salvatore's skull, making him fall to the floor. Lucia picked up a stool, and brought it crashing on top of Salvatore, making him cry out, as his gun tumbled to the ground.

"You fucking bitches!" Jimmy shouted at Stacey and Lucia, his gun still pointed at Aaron's head.

Instantly, the four men aimed their guns at Lucia and Stacey and Stacey felt Marcellus grab her from behind. She saw one of the men strike Lucia and her fall to the ground. She tried to fight against Marcellus but his grip was too tight. The bones in her hand felt like they were going to break as the rock was pushed out and then an intense pain took over her as Salvatore's fist came crashing into her face. Her body crumpled to the ground and she welcomed the feel of the cold floor against her throbbing face.

"Get your fucking hands off her!" Aaron shouted, pushing Jimmy out of the way.

Through her blurred vision, Stacey saw Aaron drop down as Jimmy struck him around the head with his gun.

"You will pay for this you fucking *puttas*!" Salvatore said, the blood dripping down his eye as he walked towards Aaron.

"Are you OK, Stacey?" Aaron called out to her as she felt her hands being clasped together with a rope.

"Yeah, I'm alright. You?"

"Could be better, sweetheart. Hang in there alright."

Stacey watched helplessly as Jimmy hit Aaron again.

"How many times do I have to beat you, before you realize I am being serious?"

"Aaron must be happy to have such loyal girls working for him. Ones who will do whatever it takes, even if it means putting their lives in danger. Can you see how manipulative your brother is, Jimmy?"

"I see it and I'm not surprised, he's always tried to control me. Well now it's your turn to be controlled big brother. Open wide." Jimmy forced his gun into Aaron's mouth.

"That's right, my friend. No longer are you gonna answer to him. All you have to do is pull that trigger and he is gone and everything you ever wanted will be yours."

The rope burned against Stacey's skin as she tried to wiggle free. Her eyes met Aaron's from across the room. She couldn't stop the tears from welling up as she realised that all he ever wanted was for her to be safe. If

280

she hadn't ignored his advice, they would have never found themselves in the situation they were in now.

"Before I kill him, I want him to tell me where he has put my drugs. He's not going to get away with robbing me. That was fifty grand's worth of stuff and I want it all back."

He pulled his gun out from Aaron's mouth.

"I promise, I didn't take your drugs, Jim, and I didn't take your girl. All we wanted to do was look after you. Your using was going to kill you, and the whole family agreed to get you help."

"The whole *fucking* family. You know mum and dad don't bother with me. Why should they, when they've got their golden boy? They'd rather see me dead than help me out."

"That's not true, Jim. Yeah, they found it hard when they realised you were using but they wanted you to come off the stuff, just as much as I did."

"Well you know what, I don't need your kind of help. I know you couldn't bear to see me making something of myself, and I know that's why you fucked up my deal at Space so screw you, screw mum and that selfish cunt Dad. All I want is my drugs back."

"How many times do I have to tell you, Jim? It wasn't me. I have no interest in messing your shit up. If you want to know who took your drugs, then look a little closer to home."

Jimmy, who had not taken his eyes off Aaron the whole time, turned to Salvatore.

"Did you order Fabs to get shot?" Jimmy asked, suddenly looking nervous.

"What the fuck you saying? I swear I'm gonna blow this motherfucker's head off. You believe him over me? After all I done for you, my friend, my brother?"

"Don't listen to him, bro' it's obvious he's lying. Think about what he would benefit from having our territories."

Jimmy rushed at Aaron, his gun pointing in his face as Stacey screamed.

"I ain't your fucking brother. Any ties I had to you, died the day you decided to put me into that hell hole and take my girl. Why would I trust you? I've got a good mind to finish you off now!"

"Do it! Be a fucking man!" Salvatore shouted, spit flying from his mouth.

"I've got no reason to lie, Jimmy. I'm going to die here anyway. I'm sorry about Fabianna, but nothing went on, you gotta believe me. Not in a million years."

"Where's my drugs?" Jimmy asked, his hands shaking as he tried to aim.

"You're making a huge mistake. It's him, he wants us all dead!"

Jimmy's fingers pushed against the trigger; unable to watch anymore, Stacey shut her eyes and prayed for a miracle.

5

"He's telling you the right thing."

Jimmy's fingers uncurled themselves from around his gun and turned around to face the approaching intruder. At over six foot, five inches tall, he towered above the rest of them as he pointed his black gun at Salvatore's head. A gang of twenty armed men marched into the room from the fire exit and the back door. They more than outnumbered Salvatore's men who, with guns now pointing at their heads, surrendered their arms. All apart from Marcellus and Alfonso, who lunged towards Lucia and Stacey, pressing their guns into their backs. Salvatore's face had gone completely white as he looked at the man in front of him in disbelief.

"Drop your fucking weapon, Nico," Jimmy commanded, standing in front of Salvatore, his trigger still aimed at Aaron's forehead.

Hearing the word Nico made Stacey look over at Lucia, who was gazing at him like he was some sort of

God. *She must have brought him here,* Stacey thought, admiring her resourcefulness. Nico spoke in Italian, his deep voice echoing across the room.

Salvatore's men looked angry as they listened to what Nico was saying and Stacey started to gather that whatever information he was sharing in the room was enough to make them see their boss in a different light.

"What the fuck is going on? Why is he pointing a gun at you, Salvatore? I can't understand a fucking word he's saying."

Salvatore remained silent, his face now twisted into an indignant sneer. The gun in Jimmy's hands started to shake.

"What the fuck is he saying?"

"Let me tell you what is going on, Jimmy. When you went away it wasn't your brother who robbed your pushers, it was us. Salvatore wanted me to rob your brother's villa and execute a hit on your girlfriend, but I refused. He planned to make a war between you and Aaron. He'd seen Aaron with Lucia and her friend in Space and wanted to make it look like Aaron had taken the drugs. He wanted to ruin you and then make you think it was your own brother. Believe me when I say that he doesn't want to help you, he just wants to use you, like he used me."

"And why should I listen to you?" Jimmy replied, still aiming his gun at Aaron, whose face had regained some of its colour.

"Because I know where he has hidden your drugs. Believe me he's a monster, he raped my fiancée days before our wedding and convinced me she had slept with someone else.

"He ruined my life and he will ruin yours."

Jimmy's mouth dropped and the gun in his hand started to flop to the ground.

"Don't you see? He manipulated me like he is doing to you. He wants you dead, he told me himself. Don't make the same mistake I did."

"Don't listen to him, Jimmy, he is a liar. Marcellus, I think we should show these mother fuckers how serious we really are. Shoot the fucking English girl."

Stacey felt Marcellus' body tense up at Salvatore's request, and knew it was only a matter of time before he pulled the trigger. She bit down as hard as she could on his hand, feeling the flesh tear against her teeth. He let go of her, and she ran over to Lucia as the sound of a gun being fired reverberated through the room. She ducked onto the ground as she heard Alfonso cry out. His body fell inches away from her as Lucia joined her on the floor. Both of them were still tied by their hands, and they crawled across the floor together in search of the exit. There was another gunshot, this time the bullet nearly hit Stacey. She glanced behind her and saw Marcellus heading towards them. Before he had a chance to shoot again, a bullet hit his chest and he collapsed on the ground. The shot had come from Jimmy, who looked at her like he was about to burst into tears. Stacey noticed two passports hanging out of Marcellus's shirt pocket and without hesitation she grabbed them with her teeth as he lay on the ground fighting for his life. There was another shot and Jimmy fell down next to her, his neck was dripping with blood. She reached over to him and he grabbed onto her, his sorrowful eyes meeting her own.

"Tell them I'm sorry. It all went too far." Before he could continue speaking, blood started spluttering from the side of his mouth. Stacey rushed over to him but with her hands still tied behind her back she was unable to tend to his wound. She could hear angry voices shouting in Italian and English. More shots were fired and she felt someone grab her from behind.

"There's nothing you can do. Leave him!"

The blood rushed back to her hands as the rope binding her wrists was loosened. She turned to face Aaron. who was now making his way over to Lucia. Taking the passports from her mouth, she crawled over to them. Aaron had managed to untie Lucia but instead of following him towards the exit, she was looking back at the carnage they were trying to escape.

"Come on, Luce. We can't stop. We need to go. Now!"

Lucia stayed rooted to the ground as a bullet whooshed past her head.

"I can't leave him!" she sobbed, her gaze still fixated on the smoke-filled air behind.

"Please, Lucia, we're going to die if we stay here."
Aaron's face was so bloodied and desperate, Lucia
reluctantly took Stacey's hand and let her guide her
towards the car park. Aaron clicked the monitor on his
keys and a white BMW bleeped in response. Stacey and
Lucia got in the back as the car screeched into action,
skidding out of the car park at top speed. The echoes of
gun fire were still ringing in Stacey's ears as she
comforted Lucia against her...

"I'm so sorry about Nico, Lucia." Aaron said, his
eyes examining them from the rear view mirror. "It just
wasn't possible for us to go back. Rest assured, my men
will be backing him one hundred percent so he'll have a
proper advantage. All you girls need to worry about right
now is your own safety. You've both been caught up in
all this shit for way too long."

Aaron switched the radio on and Mylo's, *Drop the
Pressure,* came through the speakers as his eyes scanned
the rear view mirror.

"I'm afraid we've got company, ladies. Put your
heads down."

Bullets were fired into the back windscreen, making
it smash into thousands of pieces. Lucia and Stacey
screamed as they ducked down on the floor of the car.
The car raced past the egg shaped roundabout, and onto
the hills at the back of San Antonio as it was ricocheted
with more bullets. Stacey saw a bullet penetrate Aaron's
seat and screamed his name but there was no reply. She
immediately climbed into the front and tried to grab at

the steering wheel, but Aaron's body was slumped over it and she couldn't push him back. Without anyone steering, the car went veering off the road and down a rocky verge. They hit a protruding stone, catapulting the vehicle upside down. Pain soared through Stacey's body as something impacted her head and then everything went black.

6

Stacey prized open her eyes and looked around the dimly lit room. There was a television mounted on the wall, a chair in the corner, and a jug of water with some plastic cups stacked next to it on a table adjacent to her bed. She winced as she pushed away the blankets. She was surprised to see her clothes were gone and she was wearing a paper thin robe. It all seemed rather clinical, then it hit her, *she was in hospital.* All her memories came flooding back; the shootout, the crash, Lucia, Aaron, Nico and Salvatore. She got out of bed, found her clothes on the chair and put them on. Her chest ached as she pushed open the door, but she ignored it, *she had to find Lucia and Aaron and see if they were OK.*

She peered through the door, surprised to see that there were no officers waiting for her outside. The reception area was a busy hive of nurses and doctors who thankfully didn't notice her as she exited the room. She slowly walked past the open wards, hoping to spot Lucia, whilst trying her best to seem as inconspicuous as possible. There was no sign of Lucia anywhere, and she felt the panic start to rise in her chest. She opened the door to one of the closed rooms and was confronted by an angry woman who shouted at her in Spanish. Not letting it deter her, she moved onto the next door. Inside she found an old woman encased by the sheets of her bed, she looked up at her with sad, hollow eyes but said nothing. On her third attempt, she found Lucia. She was asleep in her bed, her chest was rising up and down but there was no drip attached; breathing a sigh of relief, she closed the door and noted the number to her room.

Stacey needed to find Aaron, she was almost certain he wasn't going to be lounging it up in the minor injuries ward. She shuddered as the memory of him getting shot and then the car crashing entered her thoughts. *Had he survived?* A woman walked past in green scrubs. Stacey stopped her and asked her where the intensive care ward was. She pointed to the other side of the building. Stacey's head was pounding and her body felt like giving up, as she made the long journey over to the other side of the hospital. She nearly turned back when she spotted three policemen in the main reception area. With her head down and eyes to the ground, she kept walking in the direction of the Intensive Care Unit. She prayed that Aaron was OK, she wouldn't be able to forgive herself if anything had happened to him.

Stacey managed to walk behind a nurse and through the secured entrance of the ICU. She kept her eyes peeled for any signs of Aaron. There was drawn a man walking through the back of the ward. Dressed in a tracksuit, cap and trainers he looked completely out of

291

place compared to the doctors and nurses in their green scrubs. On closer inspection, Stacey could see he was unshaven, his eyes were bloodshot and his face was drained of any colour. She hung back and watched as he opened one of the doors, peering cautiously around him before entering.

She crept up to the window of the room. Aaron was laying on a bed; his face and body covered with tubes that the intruder was now trying to detach. Stacey ran into the room and pulled at the man's arm. He spun around and pushed her off him so hard she fell to the ground. She felt his foot kick into her and fought to catch her breath. Trying to lift herself up, she saw another set of feet almost child-like in size, adorned in a pair of navy blue espadrilles.

"Take your fucking hands off those wires, arsehole."

Stacey glanced up and saw a gun being pointed straight into the man's back. She followed the arms holding the gun. They belonged to a woman, just short of five foot, who wore pink glasses on her chubby face and whose auburn hair was pulled neatly into a bun.

"I'm sorry, Mrs Conroy. I was forced to do this. They threatened to kill my little girl."

"Get out of here now, Tony, before I decide to shoot you myself."

With that Tony ran out of the room as Stacey lay there in shock. *Mrs Conroy? Aaron's mum?*

"Fucking amateur. Come on, girl, get up, you can't be on that floor. I take it you're Stacey?"

Stacey caught a waft of Mrs Conroy's perfume as she leant down towards her. She took hold of her outstretched hand, allowing herself to be ushered to a chair in the corner of the room.

"I'm Rosie, by the way. Aaron's mum. Where's your friend, Lucia?"

"I left her asleep. I've gotta get back to her."

"Hold your horses, girl, what room's she in?"

"401 in minor injuries."

Rosie retrieved a mobile from her bag, and with the gun still in her other hand, she dialled a number.

"Frances, we need someone over here now. Bloody Tony Engles, the prick, has just tried to hit our Al. He won't have gotten far, so get the boys to hunt him down. Yeah, I got her with me now but her mate needs someone over there. Yeah minor injuries 401, don't waste no time. That bastard has his rats crawling around everywhere." Rosie closed her phone and put her gun into her bag. She took a deep breath and turned her attention to Aaron, whose chest was rising and falling steadily in time to the bleeping of the machine next to him.

"Is he going to be OK?" Stacey asked, the tears welling up in her eyes.

"I hope so, love. Luckily, that pathetic excuse for a man didn't manage to pull out any of the wires but Aaron's been hit near the spine so he's definitely got a fight on his hands.

"My poor, poor boys. Thank God you turned up when you did, 'cause I was out for the count. I haven't slept since they called me over here."

"I'm sorry for your loss Mrs Conroy. I was with Jimmy before he passed away."

"You were?"

"Yeah, he saved my life. He wanted to let you know he was sorry."

"My boy said that?"

"Yes. I don't think he ever wanted any of this to happen."

"You know, I always hoped he would find his way back to me. That stuff messed with his mind and made him an easy target for Salvatore. I should have never, never, let him out of my sight."

"You can't always be there for the people you care about, especially if they push you away."

"He thought he was on top of it all but how can you be with that stuff? If there is one thing I could wish for, it would be that my boys had nothing to do with the business but it's not that easy. You can't escape what you're born into, especially when you're a Conroy." Rosie's glasses steamed up and tears fell down her reddened cheeks. "I told him that it would end up killing him but he wouldn't listen. Now, not only have I got to bury him but I might have to bury my other boy who never done anything wrong."

"Let's just hope it doesn't have to be that way," Stacey said, putting her arm around Rosie.

"You're a sweet girl and real pretty, just like Aaron said. I know the last thing he wanted was for you to be caught up in this. The bizzies are going to want to interview you and Lucia as soon as. They won't be able to tie you in with the shoot out though. Not if I have my lawyer brief youse on what to say.

"Of course you can both stay at the villa whilst you're being held here. Then you can get off this island and start your lives over. We'll obviously be able to help you out with any of costs back home; you deserve it after everything you've been through. The bizzies will be narked to let you go, but they 'aven't got a leg to stand on, keeping you here. You girls were in the wrong place at the wrong time, that's all. Any luck and you can be off the island by the end of the week."

"I really appreciate your help, Rosie, and your offer to stay at the villa. I hadn't even thought that far ahead." Stacey couldn't stop staring at Aaron, and the machine which was helping him to breathe in and out. "It doesn't feel right to just leave him though."

"This is our Aaron's fight now, love. The quacks have given him a seventy percent survival rate, but they're still not sure if he has damaged any of his nerve endings. It's going to be touch and go for the next twenty-four hours, then we should know for sure. Al wouldn't want you here feeling sorry for him, I know that much. No doubt he'll want to see you as soon as he is better, but I need you to consider your options, Stacey. Ours is not a world you enter lightly into. Yes, we have all the materialistic things everyone could ever want, but you always have to keep your eyes open. You lose focus for one moment and this is what can happen"

Stacey looked down at Aaron and sighed, *why did everything have to be so complicated?*

"Thank you, I will definitely think about everything you've said to me. I better head back to Lucia, she'll be petrified if she wakes up and I'm nowhere to be found."

"You go to your friend love. I've got one of me men waiting close by. When you're ready to leave let him know and he'll take you to the villa. If you need anything I'm here."

"Thank you, there was one thing."

"Go on."

"I was wondering if you heard anything about a guy called Nico? He's a good friend of Lucia's and he literally saved us all from being killed back at the club. It broke her heart when we had to leave him behind."

"Nico? Sorry love but the name doesn't ring a bell. It's probably a good thing, I only know the names of the ones found dead. I'll keep a listen out and if I hear anything I'll let you know."

"OK thank you. One more thing." Stacey swallowed hard before she continued.

"Yes, go on, kiddo."

"Tell Aaron I love him please." Stacey could see Rosie force out a smile.

"In that case, I'll guess I'll be seeing you very soon then Stace."

Stacey rushed back to the minor injuries ward, praying that Lucia would still be there. She pushed open the door to Lucia's room and felt the breath leave her body as she saw a tall man hovering over her bed.

"What are you doing? Get away from her!" she shouted, preparing herself for another fight with an assassin. The man turned to her, traces of blood smeared over his face.

"Nico! You're alive!"

"Good to see you, Stacey."

"Stacey! Thanks to God! I was thinking the worse things! I looked for you but you weren't in your room and the nurse thought you might have gone." Lucia was sitting upright in bed, tears running down her face. She started sobbing uncontrollably as Stacey joined her on the bed and hugged her tiny frame.

"Are you OK, baby? You seem in pain."

"It's OK, I'm just sore from the crash," Stacey lied, not wanting to alarm Lucia by mentioning Tony and his failed attack. "What about you?"

"I'm sore, too, but lucky nothing is broken. I'm just finding it hard to swallow." She lifted up her head revealing deep purple bruises around her neck.

"Ouch, babe, you were so brave, that Salvatore is a psycho for what he did to you.

"And what about you, Nico? Did they hurt you?"

"Me? No way. I'm, *how do you say*? *Invincibile.*" Nico looked out of the window as he said it, his voice trailing off into the panorama below.

"I'm glad to hear it. Without you we would have all wound up dead. Is there any news on Salvatore? Please tell me he was one of the casualties."

"Unfortunately no. I chased the *bastardo* to Cala Longa but somehow I lost him there. My men are sure he's still on the island but I think he is gone now. I wish to God, I had been able to kill him when I got the chance. When I hear about your crash, I stop to search for him and come straight here. I needed to know you were both OK." He turned back to face them, his expression etched with concern. "And what about Aaron? How is he? Lucia say to me he was shot in the back."

"He isn't good to be honest, there's a chance the bullet may have damaged some of his nerve endings. They've given him a seventy percent chance of pulling through."

"I will pray for him, he was a hero taking you girls away from it all." He shook his head, whilst fingering the rosary beads around his neck.

"I just can't stop to think that I could have prevented all this. I knew Salva since we were children, I knew what he was capable of but I always had this loyalty to him. When he told me of his plans to take over the island, like a stupid, I supported him. I never knew thought it would involve shooting an innocent girl." Nico took a deep sigh and rubbed his hand through his hair. "I found out, after three years of marriage, why my wife refused to sleep with me. He raped her, the night before our wedding. What kind of sick person does this to his friend? You know what the worst part of it was? Somewhere, deep down, I'd known all along. There was something in her eyes whenever he would come around her. And all along I was too busy plotting ways to make more money with him to notice."

"You weren't to know *amore mio*. We were all fooled by him."

Nico took off his glasses and turned back towards the window.

"How could I not realize what he had done to her? She was my wife. I should have protected her from him."

He pressed his fist against the window and scrunched his forehead against it.

"I won't rest until he has paid for the pain he's caused."

"Hasn't there been enough fighting?" Lucia asked, her forehead wrinkling at the sides as her bottom lip quivered.

"We will talk about this another time *piccolina*. For now focus on getting better. I won't be far, OK?" He kissed Lucia passionately on the lips and stroked her face before heading towards the door.

"*Ciao amore*," she answered back, biting down on her bottom lip as she watched him leave the room.

"*Ciao amore mio, Ciao* Stacey, look after her please."

A silence hung in the air, as the ashes of what had just passed settled between them. Stacey was still on the bed next to Lucia, it was the first time they'd been alone since their argument and with so many questions she wanted to ask, she suddenly she felt awkward around her estranged friend.

"You know that I could never have lived with myself if something had happened to you." Stacey turned to Lucia whose green eyes were starting to water.

"Why, Lucia?"

"Why what?"

"Why did you feel the need to disconnect from yourself like that? To me you have it all: strength, beauty and this amazing talent. Why nearly throw it away?"

Lucia sighed and closed her eyes as her the tears rolled down her cheeks.

"You remember what I told you about Christian, my ex drug dealer boyfriend who I caught with another girl?"

"Yes, of course I remember."

"I never tell you about the men who he owe a lot of money to. They wanted to teach him a lesson he wouldn't forget. They knew the only thing he treasure was me, so when I was walking on my own one night, they kidnap me. I was kept in a dark room where they undressed me and did things I don't even wanna talk about. When they finished, they dumped me back in my home town, naked. Everyone see me, but I couldn't go to the police because of Christian. I turned into a real addict then. Christian couldn't bear the thought of what they had done and I couldn't bear for him to touch me, so he goes off with someone else. Thanks to God this happened, as it made me leave him and clean myself up. When I see how our room was trashed, I start to think that maybe something like that could happen again. I didn't want to be weak, so I start to do the coke. It helped me to escape my fear but then I got so lost, I found it hard to get back. By the time I realised what a monster Salva was, I was completely trapped. I'm so sorry, for what I put you through."

"That's terrible Lucia, I wished you'd told me about this sooner I would have understood and maybe could have reassured you."

"I couldn't even admit it to myself Stacey, I was a mess. It's not something I usually like to think of but the situation we had brought back all the bad memories."

"I need you to promise me that no matter what, you'll stay well away from that stuff in the future. I couldn't bear to lose another person I love because of drugs."

"I promise I'm never going to lose myself like that again. I won't risk my friendship with you again."

"Please don't. I can't even start to imagine my life without you in it. Not only are you my best friend but you're also responsible for helping me become the person I could only dream of being."

"I only made you realise the strength that you had inside of yourself all along. When I saw you dancing in Amnesia, I could see how much potential you truly had. Look at you now, your courage has saved us all. I'm so proud of you and the woman you've become."

Stacey could feel the tears welling up in her eyes.

"Thank you, Lucia, I certainly feel different, stronger somehow, which I think is going to come in handy. Aaron's mum, reckons the police are going to want to ask us some questions about what happened."

"We going to be in trouble?"

"She's given us her solicitor and apparently if we plead ignorance to it all, the police won't be able to hold us."

"So, we gonna have to wait here till then. I really hope Nico is right about Salvatore not being here. Just the thought of what he might do if he finds us."

"I don't think we're going to have too much bother. Not only has she given us her lawyer but we also have a team of men protecting us," Stacey said, indicating to the heavy set man positioned outside the door.

"He's for us?"

"Yep."

"OK, I'm feeling a little better for this now. What about Aaron? Is he gonna be in trouble too?"

"As soon as he comes off that machine, the police are going to want to interrogate him. The fact that he was found with a gun and shot at in broad day light, is bound to have roused some suspicions. He could even be looking at time in jail."

"Shit man, that's so bad."

"I know, Aaron's mum told me to consider my options, said his life isn't one to enter into lightly."

"This is true but I can see that you love him."

"Yeah but do I really need that in my life? I've had so much drama already."

"Sounds like you need some time to think about this one, baby."

"I really do."

"Are you hungry?"

"Ravenous."

"Let's see if our friend wants to take us to Café Del Mar. I never did get to show you the most beautiful sunset on the island."

"What about the police?"

"I'm sure Aaron's mamma can sort it out for us. For sure we need to get out of this place. As we say in Italy, no important decisions were ever made on an empty stomach. Plus, we could both do with some sun on our faces."

"You know what, that sounds like the best idea I've heard since we arrived here."

Stacey exchanged a weary smile with Lucia, grateful to have her best friend back in her life once again.

Two years later...

It was almost the weekend and *Bellissima's* was buzzing with women's chatter, music from the radio, and the various heated appliances being used. After a busy week, Stacey was looking forward to restful days ahead, she'd been feeling so tired recently. The door to the salon opened and all the women fell into a hushed silence as Aaron entered the room. He limped ever so slightly nowadays, and it served as a constant reminder of how close he had come to losing his life back in Ibiza.

"You all right, sweetheart?" he asked, as he walked towards Stacey and kissed her on the lips.

"Yep, just rounding up," she said as the ladies in the salon cooed in their direction.

"Place is heaving, you must have made a small fortune today, love."

"Yep it's been a good week."

"It's a good week every week with your brilliant business brain." Aaron winked at her and Stacey felt the blood in her body getting hotter.

"Why thank you, my darling. Are you still dragging me to that swanky bar up town?"

"You don't sound like you want to?"

"I'm just being lazy, of course I want to. I know you've had it booked ages ago."

"Yes I did, so get your best dress on and let me show you the night of your life."

"You always say that!"

"And don't I always deliver?"

"I'll go with him if you're not up for it." One of the older woman, who had her hair in rollers shouted out, causing all the women to stop what they were doing and start laughing.

"OK, OK, give me five and I'll be ready to leave."

"That's my girl, I'll be waiting in the car for ya."

The candlelit restaurant overlooking the London Skyline was breathtakingly beautiful and Stacey was glad she had worn her favourite pale pink dress and gold heels. Aaron ordered them a bottle of Laurent Perrier Rose on ice and as they both looked out at the stunning view, he took her hand within his own.

"I love you so much, my angel."

Things hadn't been easy for them; after fighting for his life, Aaron had been sentenced to six months inside Palma's jail and had banned Stacey from visiting him. Thankfully, she'd had Lucia by her side to comfort her. After Lucia and she had been permitted by the authorities to leave Ibiza, they'd rented an apartment in Hampstead near the park and both regained their employment at The Phoenix. Lucia had stayed in regular contact with Nico, who'd managed to track Salvatore to Brazil yet still hadn't managed to infiltrate his guarded headquarters. Many a night, Lucia and Stacey would find themselves sad for the men whose duty came before their own happiness.

Stacey had spent the last six months thinking long and hard about Aaron and herself. Yes, his life came with danger, but the thought of living without him was worse than any pain she could ever imagine to endure. She didn't even know if he felt the same, she hadn't heard from him since he'd been put inside, and for all she knew he could have changed his mind. The only thing she could do was get her head down and wait and see, it was beyond torturous for her.

A week after Aaron's release, he turned up on Stacey's doorstep, flowers in hand and a lighter look in his eyes. Prison had been hard on him, but it had also given him time to reflect on his situation. He'd returned to Liverpool and renounced his duties as a Conroy, causing an enormous uproar throughout his family. Lucia had also reassessed her life and decided to return to Rome to make amends with her estranged mother and father. Stacey had tracked down her own mother but she was in such a state, she hadn't recognized her at first. When she was finally convinced it was her daughter, she'd told her in no polite way to 'fuck off'. It was the last time she would bother; years of abuse and neglect had made it an easy choice for her.

It didn't take long for Aaron's parents to accept his decision; the pain of losing one son wasn't something they wanted to repeat, so they agreed to let him have a normal life and gave him money to invest into it. He and Stacey had become inseparable ever since he came to London and it was his parents' generous gift of money that had brought her the salon which she named *Bellissima's,* after her Italian friend. Lucia had decided to stay on in Rome with Nico, who had finally given up chasing Salvatore. She was now teaching ballet to children and owned a beautiful house in the outskirts of Rome with Nico, which Aaron and Stacey had been delighted to visit.

The champagne was popped open and Stacey stared wistfully into Aaron's eyes. She loved this man like she'd never loved anyone and was so grateful for their peaceful life together. Maybe it wouldn't be so peaceful anymore though, she had some exciting news for Aaron. She watched as he fiddled inside his suit pocket, suddenly realizing that for the last five minutes he had been acting very strange.

"I wanted to ask you something, Stacey. You know we've been through stuff that most couples wouldn't have to go through in a lifetime and no matter what we've come up against, you have always stood by me. Not only are you the most beautiful woman I've ever seen in my life, you're strong, brave, intelligent and you bring me so much happiness it's unreal. So what I really wanted to ask you, I mean what I'm trying to say is, will you marry me, Stacey?" He bent down before her on one knee, a sparkling diamond ring in his hand.

Stacey started to cry and nodded her head so vigorously she felt dizzy.

"Yes, yes, of course I will!"

He put the ring on her finger and squeezed her with all his might.

"Yes, baby, yes! You have made me the happiest man!"

"There is something else I need to tell you." She took a deep breath. "I'm, well, I'm pregnant!"

"You are? Oh wow, babe! That's the greatest news!" He leant into her and kissed her passionately on the lips.

"Mr Conroy?" They both looked up at the waitress, who was holding the biggest bunch of dark red flowers Stacey had ever seen.

"I didn't order any flowers," Aaron said, looking bemused at the huge bouquet.

"These were sent to us just now. Someone must have known about your special occasion, no? Congratulations, by the way." The waitress handed Stacey the flowers and walked back towards the kitchen.

"Who are they from, babe?"

"One minute, there's a label here."

"Read it out then."

"Congratulations to the happy couple. Enjoy your happiness whilst you can. S. What the fuck? Is this serious?" Stacey dropped the flowers from her hands onto the table.

"Give them here." Aaron reread the label, his brow furrowed.

"It's from him, isn't it? I thought it was all over."

"Get your coat, Stacey, we need to get out of here now."

"But what about dinner?"

"We can't stay for food love, I'm sorry. We need to leave."

Stacey nodded and looked down at the twinkling ring on her finger. With or without it, she would always be associated with Aaron and him being a Conroy was something that she couldn't escape, no matter how hard they both protested. She was stupid to think it could all be forgotten, just because she needed it to be. Whether Stacey wanted it or not, she had to face the fact that her world came with a danger, which like the sun could cause everything to turn into flames. *How bad was she willing to burn to be with the man she loved?*

The End